THE ADVENTURES OF DUNCAN AND HIS DUFFEL BAG

A Collection of Seven Short Stories ©2009

By
Trude Brooks

Artwork
By
The Little Artist in the Big Apple

THE ADVENTURES OF DUNCAN AND HIS DUFFEL BAG
A COLLECTION OF SEVEN SHORT STORIES ©2009

By

TRUDE BROOKS

Artwork

By

The Little Artist in the Big Apple 

Linda Brooks

Beautiful Books Ltd.
New York, New York

Published by Beautiful Books LTD.
BeautifulBooks4u@aol.com
Editor: Louise Baccari, Esq.
Printing History
PRINTED IN THE UNITED STATES OF AMERICA

ISBN 978-0-9715354-2-8
Library of Congress Control Number: 2009911460
Summary: Short Adventure stories about a boy named Duncan, who helps others, develops friendships with different animals, and explores the possibility of new places and ideas.
Contents of The Return of Duncan and His Duffel Bag to Talkatoo Cavern

1. Children's Fiction Adventure Stories
2. Fantasy stories about a little boy and his adventure with new friends in new environments.

Book and cover design by The Little Artist in the Big Apple 
www.outsidemywindow.com

In Memory of my son

IVAN NEAL BROOKS

whose presence, strength, and sense of humor
are missed but carried in my heart, writings,
and in the fanciful world of Duncan's adventures.

Special thanks to
Daniel Ethan Aks,
visionary and friend.

Preface

WHO IS DUNCAN?

Come read and explore the extraordinary stories of Duncan's adventures. A series of stories about a boy named Duncan. His trips to Talkatoo Cavern, Damanhur, Coober Pedy, explode with excitement. Duncan is brave and curious and has a tireless nature to succeed.

Look through my window

Then turn a page

A story awaits you

For many a day

TABLE OF CONTENTS

Preface

Children Look Through My Window

The Adventures of Duncan and His Duffel Bag in Talkatoo Cavern 1
I ~ Duncan and His Duffel Bag 3
II ~ When Duncan Meets Wally 7
III ~ Talkatoo Cavern 11
IV ~ Duncan Meets Wally's Friends 13
V ~ A Friend's Plan 17
VI ~ The Planned Journey 23
VII ~ Follow Me 27
VIII ~ Moving Along 33
IX ~ Almost Home 37
X ~ The Get Together 39

The Return of Duncan and His Duffel Bag to Talkatoo Cavern: The Golden Box 43

Coober Pedy 65
I 67
II 70
III 72

Damanhur and Duncan's Search For The Temple of Humankind 93

Freebird - A Discovery of the Planet of Air and Light 101

The Magical World Through Duncan's Eyes 107

Duncan and His Duffel Bag in the Petrified Forest 117

About the Author 128

About the Artist 129

Questions and Answers 130

POEMS

Published in "**Outside My Window**" ©2003

Catch a Falling Star 47
Life as a Pumpkin 74
Mr. Moon 76
The Sun 79

THE ADVENTURE OF DUNCAN AND HIS DUFFEL BAG IN TALKATOO CAVERN

Chapter One
Duncan and His Duffel Bag

~

The stream of bicycles excited the crowd and Duncan's eyes open with excitement as the bicycles raced by. Duncan's love for a bicycle entered his life when he was part of the cheering crowd at the bicycle tournament. At the age of five, this was his first experience of competition and he was so impressed with the speed and glory of the bicycles that from this day on, all Duncan could think about was having a bicycle of his own.

Duncan was small in stature; his red hair was cut short and spiked straight at the top of his head. His smile was friendly and he had a mischievous look on his freckled face.

When Duncan's dad taught him to ride a two-wheel bicycle, Duncan was six years old. Growing up as a little boy, without a sister or brother, Duncan received the attention from his parents of an only child.

Somehow the sight of a bicycle excited him and in waiting for that day; the day that he would sit on his two-wheeler finally arrived. His wild thoughts of flying through space, raising his bicycle above the ground, catching the wind between his eyes captivated his thoughts. His bicycle was like an airplane soaring through space and he was free as a bird.

Duncan was always anxious to learn and master new and exciting projects. Riding a bicycle allowed Duncan to experience new challenges and when he reached his seventh birthday, his dad agreed he could visit a friend and ride his bicycle to school. This newfound freedom gave Duncan independence and self-confidence.

Preparing for school was not a chore for Duncan. His striped shirt, jeans, and his Duffel Bag on his back completed his outfit. The Duffel Bag contained a peanut butter and jelly sandwich and a canteen of milk, which was his lunch, first aid supplies, his flashlight with an additional battery and an identification card stating his name and address with his telephone number. His school supplies and his books were part of his paraphernalia. Duncan made certain he was well prepared for the day ahead. Duncan liked school and looked forward to seeing all of his friends.

Saying goodbye to his mother, he started on his trip to school pedaling slowly and gradually speeding up his pace. Little did he know that today would not be an ordinary day. Usually, Duncan rode through his familiar neighborhood and waved to some neighbors who were picking up their newspapers, but today he had decided to take an alternate route to school. He would cycle through the park with its hills and beautiful green trees. The path was somewhat bumpy and curved but Duncan was having fun. He turned his wheels in and out. The glass-like lake on one side of the path glistened in the sunshine while newly flowering bushes showed signs of early spring. The dew created a pungent smell of fresh cut grass and everything seemed so perfect and complete.

Duncan then found himself pedaling faster than usual but not knowing why. Suddenly his bike swerved to one side and then to the other side. Duncan's bike was out of control and before he could slow down and straighten his wheels, he found himself flying through space. His head hit a tree and his feet became entangled in the wheels. A dizzy sensation took over his balance and Duncan was falling, falling, falling, his body spinning around, twisting and turning. When all motion stopped, Duncan found himself at the bottom of a deep, dark, wet ravine.

~

Chapter Two
When Duncan Meets Wally

~

When Duncan awoke, he realized he was up to his neck in water. He discovered a large lump on the top of his head and his arm was in pain. Duncan thought perhaps he had broken his wrist. His legs were in a funny position and they felt like they were stuck in the mud. Groggy and woozy, he looked around at his surroundings. Suddenly, Duncan was startled at the sight of a huge alligator swimming slowly towards him, with jaws wide open and ready to devour him. The alligator kept coming closer and closer.

Duncan screamed at the top of his lungs hoping that someone nearby would help him in his distress, "EGADS AN ALLIGATOR."

All he could think of at this moment was that the alligator was ready to swallow him and that he would become a prisoner inside his stomach. A sudden fear took over his body. Quick thinking, Duncan reached for his Duffel Bag which was still attached to his back and searched frantically for his flashlight which he pulled out and flashed in the eyes of the alligator, stunning him and causing him to come to an immediate stop.

He heard the alligator roar and saw his jaws open wide as he started to speak to Duncan, "My name is Wally the Walligator." Duncan was in disbelief. "A talking alligator", he heard himself say. Wally was about eight feet long and dark in color. He stared at Duncan. Duncan shook all over.

He finally gathered his thoughts together, took a deep breath and spoke in a loud clear voice. "My name is Duncan. Where am I?" The alligator replied, "You are in Talkatoo Cavern, where all who live here are animals who have the capability to talk." Duncan was terrified. The noises he heard frightened him. He decided to be strong and continue his conversation with the alligator. "Please understand that I was on my way to school when I lost my way." Wally was suspicious of Duncan but listened carefully to what Duncan had to say.

At that moment a strong gust of wind swirled around Wally and Duncan. Perhaps a storm was brewing. Duncan could only think of the worst. He was caught in a situation and could only go along with Wally the Walligator.

Duncan kept thinking of what Wally had told him. Animals that can talk! Wally was an example of a talking animal. Duncan wondered what else was in his future. This was another world. Perhaps he should have taken his normal route to school, but it was too late now. "I wish I was back home with my family. I'm sad and wet and my arm hurts." The wind whistled all around Duncan causing the dust to blow in his eyes. He could barely see in front of him, causing him to only be more frightened.

~

Chapter Three
Talkatoo Cavern

~

The cavern echoed with the eerie sounds of all who inhabited the cave. The size of the cavern was enormous and the circumference huge. The moisture and dampness of the cavern was the result of waterfalls and many lakes that formed from natural resources. This part of the cavern was known as the "Wetlands." The beautiful lakes housed exotic fish. The atmosphere in the cavern was mystical and mysterious. Hot springs bubbled and some birds sang tunes of mating. Along the waters edge, the penguins marched in unison. The beautiful pink flamingos (whose diet was mainly shrimp in order to keep their color bright) strutted about. In one corner, butterflies danced in the light of the cavern creating a beautiful image and sometimes resembling a rainbow.

Duncan looked around the cavern and was mesmerized by what he saw. Talkatoo Cavern was home to many creatures small and large, quiet and noisy. A chimp hung on a rope made from vines that grew out of the wall. Rocks and ledges of all sizes and heights provided sitting or resting places for all. A Blue Footed Boobie sat on a ledge. She watched the chimp doing somersaults while swinging from tree to ledge showing off his antics. The Boobie's elongated neck gave her the advantage of being able to see far and high above the water. She sat at a high point of the cavern and observed the other animals as they ate and played and sometimes interacted with each other. The cavern held an atmosphere of friendship.

~

Chapter Four
Duncan Meets Wally's Friend

~

Wally called out to one of his friends and a most beautiful bird appeared. "Her name is Blue Footed Boobie, but you can call her BFB," he said. Her flipperlike feet were bright blue. At her first sight of Duncan, Blue Footed Boobie stepped back. She had never seen a little boy. Duncan decided to retrieve his peanut butter and jelly sandwich from his Duffel Bag. He offered half of the sandwich to Blue Footed Boobie. Hesitatingly she examined the sandwich. She licked the peanut butter not once but many times and then bit into the sandwich. After deciding that this was surely a gesture of friendship, Blue Footed Boobie then befriended Duncan.

Another friend of Wally's appeared on the scene. Duncan's eyes opened wide. A large black and white cat stretched her back and hissed while snarling into a position of attack. Her whiskers stiffened and her eyes bulged. You could see she did not trust too many strangers.

At this time Wally noticed that there was tension in the air, and so he proceeded to show his friendship for Duncan by acting friendly and introducing The Angry Cat to Duncan. "Her name is Angora and when offered some food she immediately changed her attitude from angry to happy and not so suspicious."

Duncan now reached for his canteen of milk and slowly offered some of it to The Angry Cat. She also was not familiar with little boys. She lived in Talkatoo Cavern with her friends who were birds, fish, alligators and other wildlife. She had never tasted milk and decided to accept Duncan's offer. It calmed Angora and another friendship was formed.

Duncan was happy that his Duffel Bag was still intact.

Now that all the introductions were concluded, Wally thought this was a perfect time to discuss finding a way for Duncan to return to his home. Talkatoo Cavern was not an ideal place for a little lost boy. At that moment Duncan called out to Wally, "I have something important to discuss with you. Please help me return to my home. It is not because I do not appreciate your hospitality but I am lonesome for my family and friends." "I understand," said Wally, "and I have been thinking about a plan." "You see," said Duncan, "I am cold and wet, my arm hurts, and I have this huge lump on my head. I have met three new friends and am so confused about my future."

Blue Footed Boobie and Angora looked at each other after listening to Duncan and Wally. They both realized what was really happening. A human like Duncan could not live in Talkatoo Cavern.

Angora commented, "We are privileged to be able to have our own wonderful place to live. The Cavern is our home, we feel safe and happy here in Talkatoo. The days are warm and comfortable. The evenings are peaceful. We do not have a rainy season or extreme heat. Our friends are our family and we love them all."

Duncan listened and was so surprised to hear that all these animals lived together peacefully.

~

Chapter Five
A Friend's Plan

~

Wally was not vicious and dangerous as most alligators are but was tender and kind. He really had a good side to his nature. Wally spoke, "Duncan, I have a plan that I have been thinking about, but before we start our trip to bring you to your home, we must abide by the laws of Talkatoo Cavern and appear before our elders and the members of the board. We will inform them of our plan. If everyone agrees, we will start our journey to your home. A meeting of The Round Table will be called and we will wait for a decision from the board."

Wally left to arrange the meeting and called for the Wiz with a growl and a howl. The Wiz, whose wisdom and power and dedication to all who live in Talkatoo Cavern was known. He arrived in a puff of smoke to lead The Round Table. His long gray beard fell to the floor and his mane was course and thick. His wrinkled skin showed signs of age. His old wise eyes pierced The Round Table constituents. The halo circling his head gave off a feeling of grandeur. A beloved esteemed Wiz was respected by most and loved by all.

The sparkling crystal Round Table consisted of Wally

the Walligator, Blue Footed Boobie, Angora and several other Talkatoo Cavern inhabitants. There was Swoozie the white elephant, who arrived as soon as she heard a Round Table was called. Her grand size ears allowed her to hear across all of Talkatoo Cavern. That is how she heard she was needed for The Round Table. Her trunk was always facing up for good luck. Polar Bear was also present. He was known for his decision-making and had a fine reputation for fairness. Tarantella, whose tentacles were long and moved constantly as if she danced to her own tune, had a look of complete relaxation and control. The Wiz completed the circle. The Wiz, the revered elder with the most power, spoke. "This meeting of Talkatoo Cavern will now come to order. I asked Legal Eagle, our secretary, to grant me permission to read the most current news first instead of beginning with the minutes of the last meeting which as you know is customary." Legal Eagle flew about and then landed in his seat, squawked and then stated, "The most current news will be spoken by Wally." Wally then spoke. He bowed his head, "Revered Elder, Blue Footed Boobie, Angora and myself, just arrived from an experience which must be addressed before all. A little lost boy named Duncan was found in the cavern and a trip is planned to deliver him back to his home. We will now explain our plan and await your decision. We need your permission to administer this plan into action. Duncan, Blue Footed Boobie, and Angora will climb upon my back and I will ride them across Lake Leander to the end of the ravine until we reach dry land. We expect to encounter many vicious unfriendly animals on this trip. We will do our best to return Duncan home safely."

The Wiz sat quietly and then questioned Wally. "The changing of the seasons is an unusual time since the stars align with the opening in the ravine of Talkatoo Cavern. Is that how the little boy came into Talkatoo Cavern?" asked the Elder. Wally then spoke, "Yes, that is how we believe he fell into the cavern. We have plans to take him to the edge of the ravine and then Blue Footed Boobie will fly him home the remainder of the way."

All the members of The Round Table nodded their heads some looking up, and some looking down, and some looking worried. The Elder spoke, "Give us some time to consider your plan. Are there any additional supplies or equipment that you are lacking to insure a successful trip?" Wally replied, "Thank you, we have thought seriously about all our needs and decided we are complete with our equipment." The Wiz spoke, "A decision will be handed down shortly. Let us bring this meeting to a close." A loud bang of the gavel could be heard.

Waiting for the decision time passed slowly.

The four friends were bound together with one

thought in mind, to return Duncan to his home. Silence hovered over the group. Wally was restless. He moved his body and opened his wide mouth and then spoke, "Perhaps we did not present ourselves to The Wiz properly."

Angora shook herself and the hair flew all over. She showed signs of anxiety but comforted Wally with her words. "We support you Wally. You did your best to explain everything. Do not reproach yourself. Your expertise is faultless." Blue Footed Boobie agreed with Angora.

Finally, Duncan spoke, "Whatever decision is agreed upon, I am sure Wally, that you did your best."

Silence once again seemed to take over the mood of waiting. But all were hopeful that good would prevail.

Some eight hours passed before Wally was called before The Wiz. The elder spoke, "A decision has been reached. Your plan to return Duncan to his home has been considered and we all agree that Duncan cannot live in Talkatoo Cavern and this good deed of returning him to his home has been voted and agreed upon. We are all in accord as this is an honorable plan and we will pray for your safe return. Our members have never been faced with a problem of this magnitude. Living in Talkatoo Cavern where we have a life of our own and rules of our own separates us from the outside world. The laws in Talkatoo Cavern keep us protected and safe. We have developed friendships for each other and because of our closeness, facing such a problem with an outside situation was quite mind boggling but our decision stands and our word is law." The Wizard continued to speak and recited one of the codes of the cavern,

"TALKATOO ONE,
TALKATOO TWO,
TALKATOO THREE,
ALL SEATED WILL STAND,
RAISE YOUR HANDS,
BOW YOUR HEADS,
LOOK UP TO THE SKY."

~

Chapter Six
The Planned Journey

~

Wally was overjoyed and quickly returned to Duncan and gave him the good news. "We will start our journey as soon as possible." The four friends reviewed the plan once again.

Wally spoke, "Duncan, you can climb onto my back and holding the flashlight directly in front of me, I can ride you across the lake to the end of the ravine, and there you will see the opening and dry land." Duncan thought for a moment and then said, "How will I know where to go from there?"

Blue Footed Boobie was listening all the while Wally talked about the plan. She then began to speak, "I have an idea to add to your plan. If you would be willing to give me the other half of the peanut butter and jelly sandwich, I will accompany you guys by sitting on Wally and protecting you both with my large wings. When we reach dry land I will fly you home."

Now Angora, "The Angry Cat" as she was known, did not want to miss this new experience and adventure. She knew it would be quite a journey. "I can offer my expertise but I would like to own your First Aid Kit including the canteen with milk. I can help protect us from the ravages of rats. I will also climb on your back, Wally, to protect you on the journey home." Angora snarled and hissed to show her strength and friendship.

Duncan and Wally agreed to all the suggestions and offerings, and a bond was formed amongst the four friends. Duncan was once again happy and his hopes were high for his return home. The lump on his head still hurt, but with his arm feeling better and this new plan and his newfound friends, his future looked a lot brighter.

Wally was the first to speak, "Let us put this plan in motion. We will form a circle that includes us all, Angora, Blue Footed Boobie, Duncan and myself known as Wally the Walligator and let us promise each other to stay together until we have completed our journey. I know these waters and so this is the plan. There are some hungry predators lurking and waiting to attack us. We have to outsmart them. I will swim behind the rocks and the high grass. Blue Footed Boobie, how about telling us about your defense tactics?" "Well Wally, you are our transportation and your ideas sound logical. I can add these ideas to your plan. We all climb aboard onto your back. Duncan will be first as he lights the path with his flashlight. I will follow behind him and behind me is Angora. Your back is quite slippery so we must hold on real tight. Angora has long nails and will use them when necessary. Wally, we know that you do not move too fast and so we must be patient and vigilant in watching out in case of trouble. These waters are infested with wild and hungry predators as you have mentioned before. The rocks and leaves will help to hide our bodies and keep us as safe as possible. Our journey will begin before the sun rises and while the skies are dark with clouds. Now Duncan, you will hold the flashlight to guide our path. If you should see any suspicious characters dim the light twice and Wally will open his jaws showing his teeth and that should give us an advantage over anyone who wants to attack us."

Wally began to speak once more, "Blue Footed Boobie, if you hear or see any flying objects, spread your wings as wide as possible, because this usually produces a fierce wind and will also give us an advantage of safety and protection. The wind from your wings will blow away large bugs and bats. Angora you are next in line so keep your whiskers stiff and pointed. They can kill and stab any flying object that tries to close in our group. Your favorite snarl will also be to our advantage. Our main goal is to bring Duncan home safe and sound. Any questions will be answered now and then let us try to rest and sleep to be bright and alert for our journey in the morning. We have a new and exciting adventure awaiting us. Are there any questions?" "No," said Blue Footed Boobie, "No," said Angora, "No," said Duncan.

"Since there are no questions at this time, it seems that everything is understood by all."

~

Chapter Seven
Follow Me

~

The cool and quiet of the ravine helped Duncan and his friends relax and sleep.

When the dawn appeared, Duncan was the first to awaken. He gently touched his friend Wally who immediately stretched his long body causing Blue Footed Boobie to flap her wings. As Blue Footed Boobie moved so did Angora who had the most sensitive reflexes of all.

Wally spoke, "Are we ready?" The trio nodded their heads. Duncan positioned his flashlight and gripped Wally on his sides. Blue Footed Boobie flapped her feet and positioned her body on Wally as Angora placed her paws also around the body of Wally.

Wally was very alert and observed the ready to go signals. He started by swerving slowly in and around the rocks and bushes. The early morning gave Wally more confidence when slipping and sliding in and around the foliage. Wally was well acquainted with these waters, as this area had been his home for most of his life. Talkatoo Cavern was Wally's home and he loved its natural beauty.

All those on board Wally were very quiet and paying close attention to any strangers they might see. Talkatoo Cavern echoed hollow sounds of birds and other inhabitants. The shape of the cavern created its own whistles and funny unfamiliar noises. Suddenly a screeching wail ripped through the ravine. It echoed up and around causing Duncan to shake and shiver. Blue Footed Boobie, Angora, and of course Wally were all accustomed to the strange noises, but this was new to Duncan. This did not cause Wally to slow down. He just continued moving along.

At the start of the trip Duncan had strapped his Duffel Bag onto his back making him feel more secure. He always carried his supplies with him, and felt as if he had an old friend he could depend on. Although the bag was near empty, Duncan held onto his Duffel Bag and during the entire trip he never let go.

Wally slowed his pace for a few minutes as the additional weight of the friends on his back was not the usual he was accustomed to. Wally noticed a large rock in the distance. Sitting on the rock was another familiar face, Mr. Frog, who started to croak so loud that everyone was startled. Wally had become friends with Mr. Frog who once was attacked by a huge bat. Wally had come to the aid of Mr. Frog and he had never forgot the favor.

When Mr. Frog started to croak Wally immediately hushed him and cautioned him to be quiet. Mr. Frog was only trying to say hello and show his enthusiasm by croaking as loud as he could. His voice echoed through Talkatoo Cavern causing a restless feeling amongst all.

Duncan kept thinking how slow they moved and this disturbed him and caused him to doubt if Wally knew where he was headed. He certainly could not question Wally as it might irritate him, and so Duncan kept quiet and hoped and prayed for good results.

Suddenly Blue Footed Boobie spread her wings stretching and flapping them, for at that moment she observed the largest bat flying in their direction. She had to use all her might and force to direct the bat away from herself and her friends. Twisting and turning her wings around and around and then up and down sideways and in any direction her wings would go, she finally beat the bat off to the other side of the ravine.

Wally never ran off his course. Through this entire incident, Wally held steady and moved forward. Duncan held onto Wally, and Angora held fast in her upright position.

Wally was so happy to have Duncan holding the

flashlight as it made his eyes more relaxed and clearly showed him the path, as sometimes the water beneath his body splashed and wet his eyes, clouding his vision.

Angora felt a little restless. Perhaps her keen senses were surmising something was amiss. She was right as trouble was awaiting them. Angora rounded her back and snarled into an attack position. There, facing Wally was Mr. Rat who usually had a group of his friends with him for the sole purpose of feasting on others. Angora was smarter than Mr. Rat and did not wait. She jumped clawing and biting Mr. Rat so that he ran and ran so fast that even Wally was surprised and delighted. Wally certainly had chosen the perfect team to make this journey a success.

A total of at least two hours had passed and Wally surmised that the end of the lake and the ravine would soon be in sight. He wanted to reach his destination but he knew that all this excitement although dangerous would be over, and his friend Duncan would be back home and he would never see him again.

Now Blue Footed Boobie with her elongated neck and beak and great vision decided she would fly the remainder of the trip and look for land and the end of the ravine. Blue Footed Boobie turned to her friends and said, "We have traveled for many hours and perhaps I should now fly and search for dry land." All agreed! The words 'dry land' were musical to Duncan's ears. Wally, Duncan and Angora watched as Blue Footed Boobie made a smooth take off.

Just as Blue Footed Boobie had predicted the end of the ravine brought the journey to its first destination. All at once the reality set in that the first part of the journey was over. The friends were now forced to separate from each other and it proved to be a sad moment for all.

Duncan bent over Wally and kissed him on his slippery skin. With tears in his eyes he hugged Wally and thanked him for all his kindness and friendship and whispered that he hoped they would meet again some day.

At that moment Blue Footed Boobie appeared with the news that the dry land was close by. She then sat quietly planning the right route. When she decided where to proceed she signaled Duncan to climb upon her back, which he did. She flapped one wing as to say goodbye and they soon all were waving and off in different directions. Duncan held on tightly. The bond that had formed between Duncan, Angora, Wally and Blue Footed Boobie was soon to be over when Duncan would reach his home.

~

Chapter Eight
Moving Along

~

Angora remained on, Wally clinging to his back ready to return to the ravine. Duncan made certain that Angora held onto the flashlight for their return trip back to the murky waters and the cavern, which was their home.

Duncan gripped Blue Footed Boobie on the two sides of her hips and continued to hold on tightly. She spread her wings causing a gust of wind around Duncan. She lifted her body up towards the sky. Duncan was excited and so happy to fly with Blue Footed Boobie as she piloted the flight.

Previously she had mentioned to Duncan that on the trip home she must stop and visit three clouds. On a former trip Blue Footed Boobie had met the three clouds and a friendship was formed.

The first stop was to see Whitey, a cloud of much distinction since he was developed from a storm that had formed in the ocean and caused large and high waves with huge pockets of white foam. One pocket of foam lodged in the sky and Whitey was formed.

The second cloud was Puffy who was blown up from a windstorm at sea, and Gruffy the number three cloud, started this trio by bumping into a rain cloud by doing somersaults in the sky. Gruffy was very mischievous and would jump around in the sky causing turmoil and bumping into other clouds making it impossible to be friends with the other members in the sky. So she too formed her own private little cloud.

Duncan questioned Blue Footed Boobie about how much time it would take to reach Whitey. "It all depends on the weather conditions as the sun is hottest the later we get into the day and then I have to fly around the clouds in order to alert Whitey that I am close by and want to visit. We also must be careful not to bruise any other clouds and cause a cloudburst."

After some time had passed and enjoying a smooth ride, Duncan heard Blue Footed Boobie call out to Whitey. "Hi there!" As they entered Whitey, it seemed like they were inside a smoke screen when suddenly he motioned to them and spoke. "It certainly has been a while since we have seen each other." Blue Footed Boobie replied, "Our schedule has been full of surprises at Talkatoo Cavern keeping us close to home." The air cleared and Blue Footed Boobie flew around and in and out of the cloud and then on her way to continue their flight. Duncan thought that he had been inside a huge cotton ball and as Blue Footed Boobie flew on to visit with

Puffy, he realized that she had sat inside the cloud for just a moment and then flew in the direction of her next visit.

Puffy was close by but it seemed reaching Puffy caused a disturbance in this area of the sky. Lightning lit up the sky and so Blue Footed Boobie decided to move on quickly and save this visit for another time. Blue Footed Boobie hurried to see if Gruffy was anywhere in sight but much to her surprise Gruffy was nowhere to be found. She was so disappointed, but realized that you must not surprise-visit anyone as everyone has a schedule of their own. "Perhaps on my trip back home I can make another visit."

Blue Footed Boobie decided to continue with the planned trip and take Duncan home. A large dark cloud appeared and thunder roared and the rain soaked them both. Duncan felt his head throbbing once again and wished he were riding his bike back to school and then home.

The flight took them over trees and lakes. The houses below looked familiar and Duncan thought perhaps they were nearing his home. Just as Blue Footed Boobie started to descend to the ground Duncan shouted, "I see my bicycle lying face down on the path." Blue Footed Boobie flew closer and closer to the ground and finally landed with her floppy feet touching the ground. Her wings spread apart, which had given Duncan an opportunity to jump off and feel that he too had landed.

Suddenly his head hurt and he opened his eyes wide and looked around. He searched for Wally and looked for Blue Footed Boobie. Where was Angora the cat? Duncan sat straight up and felt the lump on his head. His heart was heavy and he felt lonely.

~

Chapter Nine
Almost Home

~

Now that Blue Footed Boobie had successfully delivered Duncan to his destination, it was time for her to return to Talkatoo Cavern, and as quickly as possible since she had to fly home alone.

Meanwhile, the trip back to Talkatoo Cavern was not as simple as when Wally and his friends helped to guide and support him.

Unbeknownst to Wally, several wild seahorses invaded Lake Leander and when they saw unprotected animals they attacked. Their large curved tail startled Angora and Wally. Their huge teeth penetrated Wally's skin. Angora scratched and stabbed at the seahorse and finally helped Wally return some wild blows with his tail.

The seahorse fled fortunately.

Just then, Duncan thought he heard voices and looked around hoping to see his friends. Then he realized that this wonderful experience about Talkatoo Cavern may have been a dream. After a few moments, Duncan's head cleared and he decided it was time to be happy and keep this adventure in his private memory because no one would believe that this really happened.

Wally and Angora finally returned safely to Talkatoo Cavern. The return trip was tedious. Wally chose his favorite lake, Lake Leander, to relax and sleep. He was always comforted by its' beauty and his fond memories. Wally knew he would have to make his friends in Talkatoo Cavern aware of the incident with Duncan, the lost boy and his journey home. The following day Wally sent a message to all that a Congressional meeting would be arranged to inform all of his most recent activities. The time would be high noon on the first day of the new month of the New Year.

~

Chapter Ten
The Get Together

~

At a congressional meeting, it was decided that all who lived in Talkatoo Cavern would attend such meetings. The day arrived and all who lived in Talkatoo Cavern emerged from their nests.

A large circle was formed and Wally placed himself at the head of the circle known as the Congressional Table. His closest and most trustworthy friends sat on either side of him, Blue Footed Boobie and Angora.

Each member who lived in Talkatoo Cavern wore an ancient coded identification tag that was created after the rocks and waters were formed in the cave. Each of the individual codes combined, held the secrets of the cavern. All who sat on the board were needed to ensure the survival of Talkatoo Cavern. The cave paintings where the codes were created and written were deep within the cavern and guarded well. Those who lived in Talkatoo Cavern never ventured into this secret area. Only Wally the Walligator, Blue Footed Boobie and Angora had access to the secrets within the cave walls.

Mr. Frog, who could be heard loud and clear, wore his biggest green jacket to the Congressional Table to ensure his ancient ancestry. Mr. Owl held a red ribbon, hooted and howled, and blinked his eyes periodically as if he was sending some type of message to Wally during the meeting. Three penguins representing the three divisions of the penguin family also sat in a straight lineup at the Congressional Table. As always they appeared clean and neat and aristocratic in their garb. The beautifully colored Cockatoo Bird positioned herself next to the penguins. One pink Flamingo Bird was a colorful sight and sat erect exuding charm. The Mere Cat jumped into her seat and the flying bat, called Fleegal, arrived and was warned to behave himself. The monkey called Mr. Senor sat quietly at the table. It was rumored that he was of South American decent. Legal Eagle abided by Robert's Rules of Order to conduct the Talkatoo Cavern Board Meeting. The Sea Horse that represented those that lived underwater swam to one end of the lake and then to the other end until he settled down. They called him Michigi.

Last but not least, the "Wiz"ard arrived to stabilize Talkatoo Caverns Congressional Table. The Wiz completed the circle.

Wally spoke with his deep majestical voice, "The meeting of Talkatoo Cavern will now come to order. I ask

Legal Eagle to grant me permission to read the most current news first instead of beginning with the minutes of the last meeting which as you know is customary." Legal Eagle flew about and then landed in his seat, squawked and then stated, "Yes Wally you may present the most current news first."

Wally began once again, "Blue Footed Boobie, Angora and myself just arrived from a journey of great importance. A little lost boy named Duncan was found in the cavern and a trip was planned and executed to deliver him to his home. All went well I am happy to say. Who else has current news?" The Mere Cat perched up on her two hind legs, raised her paw, popped her little head up and said in her sweet little voice, "I gave birth to a litter of seven while you were away and we are all doing well, at this time." She emphasized, at this time. "The changing of seasons is an unusual time since the stars align with the opening in the ravine of Talkatoo Cavern. Is that how the little boy came into Talkatoo Cavern?" Wally spoke, "Yes, we believe that is how he fell into the Cavern. We took him to the edge of the ravine and then Blue Footed Boobie flew him home the rest of the way." "I see." The inhabitants of Talkatoo Cavern listened intensely.

The beautiful pink Flamingo asked if she could bring a relative into Talkatoo Cavern. The Wiz spoke with his reverent fatherly tone, "You know we have rules forbidding outsiders from visiting Talkatoo Cavern and these rules must be abided. It is for all of your protection and for the safe existence of Talkatoo Cavern and all who live here. We have all come from a different time, and different innerlands deep within the Cavern and we must continue to respect the rules and codes and try to improve ourselves, to make a better place for each of us and the future for all generations. I wish kindness to all and please remember friendship and truth must prevail."

Wally stated with a tear in his eye, "The good deed of bringing Duncan back to his family is noted in our minutes. May Duncan never forget us and we will always remember Duncan and his Duffel Bag. Are the minutes accepted and is permission granted to bring this meeting to a close?" All agreed with a loud yes. The inhabitants started back to their individual nests and Talkatoo Cavern once again returned to its natural way of life.

~

THE RETURN OF DUNCAN AND HIS DUFFEL BAG TO TALKATOO CAVERN: THE GOLDEN BOX

The objectives of Talkatoo Cavern are to protect our animals who have shown their dedication and devotion for one another. A good deed such as the one performed by Wally the Walligator, Blue Footed Boobie and Angora when they discovered a lost little boy in the cavern and found a solution and returned him to his home is one example. With friendship and love they sacrificed themselves to find a way to return Duncan home safely. So now we once again enter Talkatoo Cavern to determine its future. We are searching for the Golden Box, which holds the secrets of Talkatoo Cavern. The caves are a sheer wonder of years gone by with a charm and beauty of their own.

Enter now and behold our precious Talkatoo Cavern. Talkatoo Cavern was peaceful and beautiful but a change in the atmosphere was on its way. Dark skies were visible through small openings in the walls and did not show much sun and light. Ice balls formed from heavy rain and bounced off the roof of the cavern. The openings above and the crevices were assorted sizes. Suddenly, the sky lit up and the walls and ledges of rock shook as if an earthquake was threatening. Could a foreign object be approaching Talkatoo Cavern? The depth of the cavern was far from the earth, a circular staircase was below the ground, and only those that lived in Talkatoo knew the exits and entrances. The approach to the vaults was miles and miles long. It was now the Year of the Dragon, and written in the scriptures was that the time was present to open and read the codes left behind by the founding fathers. Finding the codes and searching for rules and instructions for the future years created order and avoided chaos for the inhabitants. The time was now. The day had arrived. Some carried lanterns, others carried torches, and the flicker of all these lights formed a rainbow that created a warm and close feeling of companionship. Suddenly the marching crowd came to a halt. All attention was drawn to the loud rumbling noise of huge doors opening. There, high on the Stone Mountain, sat The Wizard, Sir Regal, The Elder. Silence prevailed.

Suddenly, Wally speaks. His voice resounding loudly throughout the cavern, "An audience is requested before The Wiz." Wally then bowed his head and wiggled his tail. Famous words were spoken by The Wiz. **TALKATOO ONE, TALKATOO TWO, TALKATOO THREE.**

The Wiz raised his hands above his head and suddenly red flames of fire enveloped his body. A dragon known as Frumpke appeared on one side and his jaws opened wide to show his fierce strength. On the other side of The Wiz, another dragon known as Fiddlehead appeared. Their fiery presence demanded respect. Both dragons were so gigantic in size that they created a fearsome sight. The fish in the lakes scurried about. The balcony in the cavern housed chimps who were now swinging from one height to another and quietly observing everything around them. The bat who usually flapped his wings swooshed and swayed and paid attention to all around them. Butterflies of all colors perched themselves on leaves, waiting and watching. The waters in the lakes were no longer calm and serene. The Wiz finally addressed his followers –

This is our motto.

CATCH A FALLING STAR

A Star;
The light I see from my window must be coming from a star.
It shines so bright,
It lights the night,
Yet coming from afar.
This star is not the only one,
the sky is full of stars.
They form a picture in the sky
to tell a story from on high.
Look up, look up and see this sight of
nature's miracle of the night.
For each and every star above,
a wish is born,
some out of love.
To wish on a star is to tell your dream. To the secret
light in the unknown night.
The blue of the sky is the home of the stars.
They gather together and brighten the sky,
so take a good look,
before they pass by.

The winds howled above and suddenly the sound of rain was heard. The rumbling noises caused Wally to shout "Jacaranda." The Wiz spoke, "Behind the huge doors are the vaults that hold the codes of Talkatoo Cavern. The iron doors which, when opened, lead to the steep stone steps which was a lower level to the mysterious vaults and alcoves."

Lights flashed, hot steam exploded and a cascade of water sprung high in the cave. Above and beyond some shapes appeared. A huge box lay on the floor with symbols to the tombs. **TALKATOO ONE, TALKATOO TWO, TALKATOO THREE.**

The huge green doors, which showed signs of movement, caused the walls of the cavern to shake. The birds screeched, while all who were in the safety of the cave shook with fear. Wally stood in front of the doors and looked for his familiar hiding space and also felt anxiety. Although this procedure of entry took place only once a year, no one looked forward to this day.

Today, The Wiz had spoken and all listened. "A secret was withheld from all. We have located Duncan and he has been chosen to travel beyond the green doors and open the vaults. Duncan, Oh Duncan appear and let us welcome you." Suddenly, from a large opening in the ceiling of the cavern a figure on a bicycle is seen. "It is Duncan! Although Duncan comes from another land his true nature of returning to

Talkatoo when contacted by his friends Wally the Walligator, Angora, The Cat, and Blue Footed Boobie has proved his friendship and appreciation when he was returned to his home after falling into our cavern. Duncan has been chosen at this time by our distinguished members to be the All American Talkatoo Boy. He will follow the plan and search the vaults." As Duncan approaches The Wiz, he dismounts his bicycle.

The Wiz instructs him to kneel on the floor. Now, The Wiz raises a cup filled with a steamy potion. He speaks, "Duncan you have been chosen to represent the inhabitants of our cavern. This is your task, drink this potion inside this cup, and the Gates of Talkatoo will then open for you. Beyond these gates are the future of our beloved home and further instructions for our well being." The time was set for Duncan to drink the potion. Duncan was not prepared for this. He thought to himself, I do not know what this can do to me. But I must trust The Wiz. He is our revered elder. Duncan raises the cup to his lips and swallows the contents. Duncan looks at his friends and all stood silently waiting to see the outcome.

The audience included all who lived in Talkatoo. BFB held her breath in anticipation; Wally stretched his fins and Angora the Cat, stood straight up almost out of her body with whiskers like knives. Swoozie, the white elephant, looked larger than life. She shook her enormous body. Duncan looked at his friends. All stood silently waiting to see the outcome. "Something is definitely happening to me from the top of my head to the tip of my toes."

The Wiz begins to speak to Duncan, "When entering behind the doors a ship that flies awaits you. Do not be fearful. It will take you to a destination that you never imagined beyond the sky and there lay the answers in a place called Angel Land." And so it was. The huge iron doors were now ajar and as The Wiz said, the largest flying object shaped like a bicycle stood with colored wheels, bright lights, and a dashboard with signals. The steering equipment had handles made from a tree trunk and the seat was made of black glass. The hood of the ship was shaped from a cloudy thick frosty white glass. Duncan, amazed at what he saw was now anxious to start his journey. He was ready. Duncan turned to The Wiz. The Wiz raises a cup filled with another steaming potion.

"Duncan, this is a tedious and difficult endeavor, but all together we will prevail. There will be moments of doubt for success but we are all confident in your strength and wisdom. On this dangerous journey you must survive all obstacles. A dragon spits fire and walks underground. An octopus with tentacles that kills, bars the way. The temptation not to relax and remain loyal to the cause will show in the success of your task. The future of our destiny and the strength of our existence will be shown when you succeed. You must find the golden box with maps and instructions. The tabloids were last seen in the possession of the one and only Dragon Fly from Pipers Glen. These were the scrolls that held the codes of Talkatoo Cavern. He had stolen the scrolls. His reputation for hiding in the Tunnel of The Unknown brings anxiety to all. He steals from all and hides his wares in golden boxes. Many have searched for the scrolls only to be disappointed by finding false copies. This tabernacle of wisdom must be saved. They were first discovered by the son of a hero. They have both departed to an unknown world, leaving behind this Mountain of Hope. You must find the golden box and the maps with instructions so that the good deeds may be accomplished. You will then be the one to open the vaults that hold the secrets to Talkatoo Cavern." The Wiz bows his head and looks up to the sky and stars, and softens his voice. "I hand you this ancient encrypted cup molded by our ancestors. The steam which roars out from the potion now requires that I add a second liquid to the existing potion to make it work properly." Duncan takes a deep breath, looks up to the sky and swallows quickly then yells, "I feel a surge of strength taking over my body." Duncan looks around at his friends. All stood silent. "Something is definitely happening to me from the top of my head to the tip of my toes." Duncan's outer features started to show changes. His red spiked hair took on a glow of yellow, pink and blue, his eyes bulged almost out of his head, his chest became expanded and his legs showed muscles that made Duncan look like a superhuman being. "I am ready to make my friends at Talkatoo proud of me. I will now board the bicycle ship but first I must place this magical helmet on my head." All watched and waited for the moment of departure. Duncan climbs aboard the bicycle. In a flash the motor roared, the space ship left the ground and soon was out of sight behind the doors. The ship flew at a high speed that led Duncan wondering if it could ever slow down and land.

After traveling for what seemed to be an instantaneous moment in time, Duncan saw a smooth patch of land with beautiful trees, and colorful flowers and bushes, so green. Duncan decided that this had to be Angel Land and so he slowed down by pulling on the breaks and a beautiful landing took place.

A noise of rattling and roaring suddenly enveloped the air. There before Duncan was a dragon of monumental size whose actions towards Duncan did not look friendly. Duncan stared at the dragon and the dragon returned the stare at Duncan. Duncan turned to the dragon slowly and cautiously, "Hey, my name is Duncan and I am on a mission searching for a golden box stolen from Talkatoo Cavern. This box holds important information on the future of Talkatoo Cavern. Can you help me?" Duncan during this time keeps thinking, I hope that I can befriend this dragon. Duncan keeps the dragons attention by continuing the conversation. "I must locate the golden box, with the scrolls and maps. There are directions for me to return it to Talkatoo Cavern."

Suddenly a ship lit up the sky. It did not resemble Duncan's ship. This object has large wings surrounding its body. It created a wind that blew fire and sand into the area below. The door opened and a giant sized Bubble floated into space. The Bubble floated in air and resembled a sunburst. Suddenly a loud burst resounded. The dragon stepped back looking curiously at the Bubble. Duncan also did not know what to expect. Out stepped an alien resembling the sun. His color was red hot, his eyes bulged, and he had a frown on his face. He spoke slowly, "Who is invading our land? New creatures such as you are not welcome!" Duncan for the second time in his life was faced with a weird and frightful situation, but his former experience helped him to cope. "My name is Duncan and I have only come to find the golden box. My visit here is friendly. Can you direct me to my destination?"

The Bubble spoke. "If I help you, you must endure three adventures. One, you must swim in the rapids that may turn you upside down. Two, you must fight a rattlesnake until you capture him and you must play a tune on a kazoo that reaches all the animals in Talkatoo. If you complete these three tasks, there at the end of the rocks you will find the golden box hidden underground. Now decide on your future because I must return home, as it is time to blow little bubbles in the air and make some new family." In a moments notice the Bubble disappeared but his voice is heard in the distance. "You will contact me when all three chores are completed by taking a long deep breath and blowing three times on the Kazoo. I will then return and we will discuss the golden box." Duncan turns to the dragon. "Can you help me? If you help me succeed with my three tasks on my return to Talkatoo Cavern, I will recommend that you become a talking dragon. The Wiz will consider you a friend and you will have earned a voice. You will then speak and be allowed to live in Talkatoo Cavern." The dragon could not believe that Duncan could give him a voice and make him talk. "Are you sure you can give me a voice so that I will be able to talk? If so, I will accompany you on your journey and will protect and shield you from future harm." So Duncan had once again made a new friend. "Yes, I can assist you to obtain a voice to talk, my new friend. I believe that your ability to spit fire can shield me from harm. And you then can perhaps learn to live in peace and tranquility in Talkatoo Cavern. The journey will begin as we are all ready." The dragon speaks, "Duncan, I am Frumpke and my brother Fiddlehead is my sidekick. We live and cope with problems as a team. Tarantella the Octopus has been a close neighbor and so we need the help of Fiddlehead to try and convince Tarantella of the importance of your mission so as not to cause any further problems. Let us call upon Fiddlehead who is meditating. "Brother, please come out of your trance and meet a new friend!" With a loud roar a dragon appears blowing fire. Frumpke explains the situation to Fiddlehead. "This is my new friend Duncan from Talkatoo Cavern. Please be friendly as he needs our help and expertise to make a conquest with Tarantella." Frumpke turns to Duncan. "Fortunately, Fiddlehead is in a friendly mood. He likes to be called upon for his strength and sometimes deadly tactics." "Fiddlehead, if we help Duncan we can gain our own permanent voices and live in Talkatoo Cavern. Duncan has to complete several tasks to reach the golden box as it is essential for the future well being of Talkatoo. Our work is cut out for us." "Frumpke, I think you have convinced me so let us try to find Tarantella. She usually is down under in the deepest water in the lagoon. Let us swim around and find her."

"I will wait here for you while you go to swim in the lagoon to search for Tarantella, says Duncan. What if Tarantella is not friendly to the tasks that I must complete?" Worried and fearful Duncan tried to be positive and strong and think only of the best outcome. Some time passes, then suddenly the flapping of tentacles could be heard. "Duncan, it is us, Frumpke and Fiddle Head. We are returning and have located Tarantella who is with us. Tarantella speaks, "My two dragon friends have explained your plight. What will you do for me if I help you?" Duncan quickly replies, "I can promise you three rewards, one is to give you an introduction to our future contest in Talkatoo Cavern and the other is to be able to dance with the stars at the celebration. These two prizes will make you happy. To be able to be a permanent inhabitant of Talkatoo Cavern you will gain more friends and your dragon friends Frumpke and Fiddlehead will be welcome at Talkatoo forever. Tarantella then thought and shook her head as to say yes. "I will cooperate with you and your friends. The rewards sound great, and I would have a new place to live and an entry to contests. It is certainly time for me to make a change."

Duncan recounts his three required adventures to the brothers. "I must swim the rapids that are so dangerous, fight a rattlesnake and capture him, and I must play a tune on a kazoo that reaches all at Talkatoo Cavern." The group listened intensely. Frumpke immediately tells Duncan of the ropes he owns and that he can tie them to Duncan as he enters the rapids. They will extend for many, many miles and then fall to land while attached to Fiddlehead and myself. We will then guide you safely to land. The rattlesnake in question lifts his head out of the leaves and bushes only when he hears a noise. "We must cover his head after cornering him and you can then give him the choke-hold taking care of your second feat. The third and quite tricky task is finding the kazoo." Frumpke speaks, "I must approach our musical friends the Top Notch Hot Shots and convince them that the playing of the kazoo is for a good cause. They all go to the edge of the rapids. Frumpke tells Duncan, "Now you must jump into the rapids and to balance you I will tie the ropes onto one side of your body until you can swim and hopefully be strong enough to stay on top of the rapids." Duncan waited a moment, took a deep breath and dove into the water. The rapids were cold and the current was strong and difficult to swim in but with Frumpke balancing him it made staying afloat a little easier. The currents took him up and down and the waves sometimes covered his head. Duncan thought to himself, "When will I come to the ends of these rapids?" Suddenly the waters calmed and Duncan found himself in a beautiful lake. Frumpke yanked on the rope and Duncan swam safely to shore. They threw themselves on the ground with Fiddlehead right behind them. Time to rest before attempting another dangerous feat. While Duncan rested he thought to himself, "What do I know about rattlesnakes?" This is my next task. Rattlesnakes are slippery and dangerous. Their tongues spit venom that is poisonous. I will have to outsmart the Rattlesnake by luring it in my direction, then turn him about, cover his head, and embrace the snake in a choke hold, and then return it to the Bubble. This is my plan." Frumpke and Fiddlehead agreed to help Duncan find a snake at the end of the rapids. The end of the rapids where the lake appeared did not look as if it housed snakes. Perhaps in the brush of the woods ahead, there hiding in the leaves would be a live snake. Frumpke and Fiddlehead looked to see, and listened to hear some movement in the bushes. Onto the left some leaves showed movement. Three friends held their breath in anticipation. Gliding around in and out of the brush, Duncan saw a snake searching for food. Quickly Duncan takes his Duffel Bag and throws it over the snake's head. There holding it close to the ground, the snake wiggled and hissed trying to free himself from Duncan's grasp. The movement of the snake slowed as Duncan held the snake. Fiddlehead and Frumpke came to

Duncan's side and asked "Is the snake moving? We must place the snake in the Duffel Bag so on our return we can show the Bubble the snake." The snake lay still and all three waited for any further movement. Frumpke searched the woods and came back carrying an old, large bird's nest, empty and deserted. There they put the snake inside, covered it with leaves and tied it to the Duffel Bag on Duncan's back. The trio knew that it was now time to search for the tree where the Hot Shots lived. Frumpke said, "It is time to borrow the kazoo from the Top Notch Hot Shots. Now we're off on an excursion to find my musical friends. I know that they are not far away. They usually sit up in the highest tree so as not to be disturbed when they are writing new music." Suddenly, they hear the sound of a banjo, tambourine and a kazoo. Now, Fiddlehead knows where to find the trio. "Hey big shots! It's Frumpke. Listen carefully. I have come to borrow the kazoo to help a friend in need. I hear your music. Remember when I helped you out when you were trapped up in the tree? So now please return the favor. I am going to stand up straight and you can put the kazoo in my mouth. I will return the kazoo to you at the earliest possible time."

The Top Notch Hot Shots yell down in harmony. "You must return the kazoo as soon as possible as we have certain commitments to play here in the woods. We will attach a string to the kazoo and lower it down." Frumpke calls back, "Thank you. I promise to return the kazoo as soon as my friend Duncan's task is completed."

Duncan asks the group, "What songs should be played at Talkatoo?" They thought awhile and then Frumpke and Fiddlehead suggest by singing, "How about, Friendship Friendship, nothing like a friendship, when other friendships have been forgot, ours will still be hot, yada yada yada yada yada ya ya ya." (notes) All Agreed. Then Duncan looks up at his two new friends and speaks, "Let us return to find the Bubble and tell him of our success." Carrying the snake in its container and having Fiddlehead and Frumpke as witnesses to Duncan's swimming the rapids, and with the kazoo in hand from the Top Notch Hot Shots gave Duncan a feeling of accomplishment.

Duncan prepares his friends, "I must now call for the Bubble with a blast from the kazoo to let the Bubble know that we are ready to see him, **ooooooohhh, oohhhhhhhh-hhh, ooohhhhhhhhhhh**."

Duncan turns to his friends, "Now we have to wait for the Bubble to return to the woods and receive instructions on finding the Golden Box. Frumpke and Fiddlehead, you look tired. Let us rest a while. We have been traveling for many hours. The location for the Bubble to return is about here. I remember that large rock." "We agree, let us make this our resting place."

After several hours a large gust of wind and rustle of the trees awoke the trio. Frumpke roars out, "Perhaps it is the Bubble approaching!" Fiddlehead and Duncan stand and look up to the sky. There in the distance and approaching them they saw the Bubble. With much noise and wind the Bubble landed. Duncan spoke to the Bubble, "I have the snake." Frumpke and Fiddlehead look at the Bubble and state, "Duncan had great victory in the rapids." Duncan was anxious to complete his mission and speaks up, "I will now play the kazoo. The tune is friendship and Frumpke and Fiddlehead will sing along."

Everyone appeared happy. They saluted and marched to the tune. The Bubble was impressed and ready to talk about the Golden Box. The Bubble speaks and says he is finally satisfied to tell all. "I am impressed. You have done exceptionally well and I have a surprise for you." With these words he took some deep breaths and blew many small bubbles, then a larger bubble appeared and as it burst open, the Golden Box fell to the floor. "Here is your reward. The Golden Box, cherish it with love and safety. Bring it to The Wizard and he will open it and find your future for Talkatoo Cavern."

Duncan's eyes lit up and opened wider than ever and said, "I do not know how to thank you enough Bubble," but before he could say a word the Bubble disappeared. Frumpke, Fiddlehead and Duncan look mesmerized. "Now we must return the kazoo, return the snake to his home and return to Talkatoo." The three friends turned about and started back to the Top Notch musicians.

Frumpke speaks again, "There is a hole under the brush on the left for us to return the snake." And so it was. "Now that we have accomplished that lets get back to the Hot Shots. I hear their music resounding from their tree. Duncan, tie the kazoo onto a rope and raise it up." Frumpke calls out to the Hot Shots, "I am back to return the kazoo with my brother and friend Duncan." Duncan, Frumpke, and Fiddlehead chime in together, "Thank you, we owe you one."

Duncan, relieved, speaks to the two dragons, "Our journey is half over. Let us return to Talkatoo. I must bring you before The Wizard to receive your voices and an invitation to become members of Talkatoo Cavern. Your expertise on this trip is commendable and I am so happy to have made some new friends. You will be greeted by all at Talkatoo Cavern."

Over the hills and through the tunnels the trip home was long and tiring but the three friends were so anxious to reach Talkatoo, that they persevered on. Climbing the rocks and ridges brought Talkatoo Cavern closer and closer. Duncan's bicycle held the three on the trip home. As the sunset turned to dusk the ravine came into sight. Duncan speaks, "My friends, we are now in the land of Talkatoo.

Another short distance and we will enter the cavern." And so it was. Frumpke and Fiddlehead were astonished at the inside of Talkatoo with its beautiful lakes and birds singing and animals of all kinds living together as they had never seen the cavern before. "I must call for The Wizard." Duncan bows his head and loudly says the magical words, "**Talkatoo one, Talkatoo two, Talkatoo three**. Revered elder please appear. I am Duncan and have returned with my friends carrying the Golden Box. I have with me two new friends who accompanied me with my tasks on a safe return. I have promised them voices and a life in Talkatoo. Revered elder, The Wiz, I am at your service."

The three friends stood quietly waiting for The Wizard to appear. Flashes of fire and light, a burst of thunder, and there in a flash stood The Wizard. The Wizard spoke slowly and his voice echoed through the cavern, "Tell me of your success or failure." Duncan turns to The Wiz, "Dear elder, we have good news, our journey brought success, we have the Golden Box, unopened. We retrieved it from the Bubble whose possession it was in. These are my two new friends Frumpke and his sidekick Fiddlehead. They were instrumental in my success. I would be happy if we could reward them on my behalf. If they could have voices and be allowed to come to Talkatoo and mingle with our family, they would be in debt to you."

The Wizard looked up to the sky. The Wizard spoke,

"Our motto, 'Catch a Falling Star' will soon deliver two voices for Frumpke and Fiddlehead. They have shown friendship and love." With that, The Wiz raised his wand, and tapped Frumpke and Fiddlehead on the shoulder, which showed acceptance into Talkatoo. Duncan bows his head, and hands the Golden Box to The Wizard who immediately says, "A celebration is in order. Duncan, bring the news into Talkatoo to all our family. We will all join together and enjoy our victory."

There will be music by the Top Notch Hot Shots. The chimps will sing abadabadoo. Different foods will be served. Speeches will be heard from each animal kingdom. The dress code of Mr. Frog will be his Ancestral Green Tuxedo. Blue Footed Boobie will have her toenails painted blue for the occasion, and Angora will sport a Big Bow on her collar. As a tribute to Duncan, the Top Notch Hot Shots musicians will take requests from all the animals, and Penguins will carry trays of vegetarian food. Wally will speak about Duncan's victory, and thank you notes to all who participated. Three voices on diplomas will be handed out to Frumpke and Fiddlehead.

Horns blew and whistles could be heard "Come get together. Let the dance floor feel your leather." The Hot Shots were playing their tune, kissing and hugging, singing and dancing. The celebration was in full swing. Duncan was so proud of his accomplishments, watching his friends enjoy the fruits of his labor. The chimps swung from rope to rope, singing abadabadoo. Wally the Walligator tapped his tale to the tune of the music, Angora the Cat screeched and meowed, BFB clapped her feet together making a wishy-washy noise. Mr. Frog croaked with joy, and Swoozie the white elephant shook from side to side. The festivities were enjoyed by all. The penguins marched in unison. Veggies and fruit from the trees were served to all. The time had arrived for the presentation to be given to the new friends Frumpke and Fiddlehead. The Wiz called for the attention of all by starting the fireworks and lighting up the cavern. "We are here to complete Duncan's promises. Two new voices are to be distributed. A diploma with a written scripture is awarded to Frumpke and his sidekick Fiddlehead. Please step up and accept your diploma, which is a pass to enter and live in Talkatoo Cavern. Your exceptional friendship has earned you these privileges." The Wiz handed each new member a diploma and congratulated each one. "You are now part of the Talkatoo family, and we hope to be friends forever." The Wiz approached Duncan. "I wish to present you with this medal of love from all your friends at Talkatoo Cavern; you are also part of our family." Duncan knew his work at this time was completed at Talkatoo.

COOBER PEDY

Chapter One

~

Duncan on his flying bicycle machine returned to Talkatoo Cavern. An audience was called before The Ohm to whom Duncan would present the Golden Box. The cheering crowd of friends gathered for the occasion. The Ohm appeared and Duncan knelt before him and handed him the Golden Box. They all waited with baited breath as The Ohm opened the box.

There inside were two scrolls with written instructions for the future of Talkatoo Cavern.

The number one scroll was read aloud by The Ohm. "Duncan, a magical opal of great wealth and importance awaits you. A trip to Coober Pedy in the outback of Australia houses the opal mines where the great lost opal must be found and returned here to Talkatoo. You alone must decide when and how you will accomplish this important task." As always, Duncan made a quick decision. He could never forget his friends of Talkatoo Cavern. Duncan once agreed to do his best. Never to forget when he was lost in the ravine of Talkatoo and Wally-the-Walligator, Blue Footed Boobie, and Angora befriended him and found a way to bring him home.

Duncan had never heard of Coober Pedy, Australia. He

decided to research in his most informative book called the Wikipedia. There he would find all the information about Coober Pedy and how to start the journey to find the lost opal.

To enter the world of Wikipedia was like finding lost treasures in lost corners of the world. Duncan never mentioned the Wikipedia to anyone but had it safely tucked away in a secret compartment in his Duffel Bag and when in need of help, he would turn to his Wikipedia.

When he left Talkatoo he took out his Wikipedia and searched and found what he needed. Coober Pedy was called the home under the range. Filmmakers had long used the place to portray a nuclear strike zone. Still it had a zany charm for a desert mining town.

Way out in Australia's outback where the lakes are salty and beer is warm, men with big arms and funny hats cooked kangaroos and crocodiles. River races were run in glass bottom boats. It was a weird place.

Duncan was interested, as Coober Pedy was known for its underground mines where all the opals were buried. The town had opal mines, opal caves, opal factories and an opal center.

The information Duncan found would be useful in locating and finding the lost opal. He now had to find transportation to Coober Pedy.

The Wikipedia informed Duncan to search for a vessel to make the trip. Duncan decided to bicycle down to the beach and look for a boat leaving for Australia. His trusty flying bicycle was ready to take him wherever he decided to go. The beach seemed a likely place to find a ship that was headed for Australia. When Duncan arrived at the beach he was happy to see that the ocean waves were calm but covered with whitecaps. There were many boats of all sizes docked at the beach. Duncan arrived when the sun was hot and bathers were few. Carousing the beach, Duncan noticed a vessel with a sign reading, **"Come Aboard and Sail the Sea, An Experience Awaits You, FREE."**

~

Chapter Two

~

A burly rough looking man with a beard and weather beaten face stood on the boat. Duncan approached him. "Can you tell me something about the trip you advertised? Where is your destination?" asked Duncan. "I am headed for the outback of Australia. My name is Captain Crook. I have three others on board who are making this trip with me. One, a cook, another, the maintenance man, and the other, is a weatherman. What can you do to earn your trip?" said Captain Crook. Duncan thought and finally replied, "I have an amazing flying bicycle, and as soon as we reach land, and our destination, I can transport you to all of your points of interest." Captain Crook thought to himself now I can have private chauffeur. The thought pleased him. "Done Deal." "What is your name?" "My name is Duncan and I must inform you, I am searching for a lost magical opal to return to a magical kingdom called Talkatoo Cavern." Duncan asked, "Are you familiar with Coober Pedy the opal mining town?" "Yes," said Captain Crook. "That is our main port of destination. If all is agreed on, let us plan our trip and come and meet our crew."

Duncan was excited and stepped down into the galley where Princess Pumpkin was cooking meals for the crew. Santiago was also with Jose and this team worked together. Captain Crook called to all who waited patiently to meet

Duncan. "Duncan, say hello to Princess Pumpkin our chef, Santiago our maintenance man, and Jose a former golf pro."

Doo Da was nowhere in sight. "Now Duncan," said Captain Crook, "you have met the crew and know of their background and wishes for their future. Princess Pumpkin and Santiago want to find some opals. Jose heard the golf course had no green grass and was anxious to see that." All shook hands, Santiago tipped his hat and Jose welcomed Duncan aboard.

~

Chapter Three

~

Santiago the owl had lived in a small town in Mexico, but wanted to see the world. Jose, the puppy golfer came from the USA and was ready for a new experience. Princess Pumpkin left the farm called Pumpkinville with the hope of finding some happiness. Doo Da, the parrot from Mama Rosa's house, flew the coop.

Santiago was an owl with an unusual lust for change. So he decided to leave his home and follow his dream to find new places and perhaps new friends and a different life. "I want to see the world." Santiago thought to himself. "Perhaps I can find another future for myself." His thoughts excited him and created desires, but he was also fearful and hesitated as this was a new adventure for him. He would be alone for the first time but he made a final decision and left his home.

Santiago walked many miles and suddenly came upon a peddler with a wagon full of junk. He approached the peddler. Perhaps I can help you pull your donkey with all your heavy wares. I would ride with you and you could rest. The peddler looked at Santiago and decided that perhaps this owl could make his trip easier. Santiago waited for an answer. "I am not going too far but you are welcome to ride this short distance with me." Santiago jumped onto the wagon. A part of the way he helped the peddler pull the donkey when the donkey would slow down. After traveling some distance, the peddler brought the wagon to a halt. The peddler spoke, "You must now leave me and my donkey. I am going no further." They had reached a fork in the road, which branched out into three different directions. The peddler told Santiago, that he had now had to make a choice which road he would continue on his journey. Santiago looked down and around at the three roads. He took his suitcase and stepped down from the wagon. He now had to decide. There he saw a road to the right, one to the left, and one that took on a straight path ahead. The one road to the right looked winding and narrow. The road to the left was full of holes. The center road was straight and looked more inviting. Santiago thought and finally made his choice. "I will follow the straight path ahead." He thanked the peddler for his friendship and started his walk not knowing what his destiny held for him. In the town of Pumpkinville housed a large farm full of pumpkins waiting to be picked for Halloween. The center of the farm held all the choice pumpkins. The most beautiful was called the Princess Pumpkin. There in the fields stood a sign that read, **Life As A Pumpkin**.

LIFE AS A PUMPKIN

When I was just a little seed
My head was in the ground
It took some time to pop my stem
And see what was around
A field of stems was spread across
A space for miles and miles
I grew to be nice and round
A lantern to light
A pie to eat
I ward off bad spirits for Halloween
My color is orange
My visit is short
But I'm so much fun when kids dress up
And witches howl
That time in October when we trick or treat
Remember the pumpkin it's sweet to eat.

Halloween is a celebration and the pumpkin is the main event.

Princess Pumpkin did not want to leave the farm with a new family and be baked into a pie. She hid behind the biggest pumpkin and when everyone went home and it was dark, Princess Pumpkin left the farm and walked towards the road. She walked for many, many miles and then saw a figure ahead in the dark. The princess walked faster until she was right beside Santiago. "Hello, my name is Princess Pumpkin." Santiago tipped his hat. "What is your name?"

"My name is Santiago, and I am looking to find a new future. I have decided to change my life. I have left my home." "Can I come along with you? I too am seeking a new future." "Then, follow me," said Santiago. The two, so different, soon became close friends and planned a trip together. They walked so far and were finally exhausted and fell to the ground. They slept for many hours. The following morning they continued on their way. They skipped and sang songs that they had learned at home.

Suddenly, a golfer with a green cap and carrying a green golf club, befriended the two. "Where are you two walking?" "We are off to find a new future." "I am also tired of this golf life. Can I join you two? My name is Jose. What is your name?" "My name is Santiago, and this is Miss Princess Pumpkin." Princess Pumpkin looked at Santiago and he returned the glance. "Why not?" "Follow me," shouted Santiago. Now they were a trio.

The road was long and dusty. There were hills and dales making it difficult to walk. The three were getting hungry. "What can we do?" Santiago said, "Well, I packed some food before leaving my home. If it pleases you both I will share it with you." He opened the package and there low and behold was a pizza. "Hey guys, help yourself. Sharing is important amongst friends. We must all help each other." Santiago, the Princess, and Jose sat in a circle and enjoyed the food. After a nice lunch they continued their journey.

Just ahead they saw a beautiful beach with white sand, and there the oceans waves were rolling onto the shore. "Let's go for a swim," said Santiago. "We can jump into the waves and swim together." After enjoying the water, the three laid down and fell asleep. When they awoke it was no longer daytime. There was a full moon shining and Santiago remembered a poem he had learned.

MR. MOON

Mr. Moon with your smiling face,
What do you see when you look down on me.
When I look up and see the sky
You are far away
You are up on high
I wish I could touch you
I want to be close
To know you better
To be your friend
To know what you're made of
To know what you think
You're a friend yet a stranger
So high in the sky
I'm here on earth for this is my home
You're up in the heavens that's where you roam
Oh, Mr. Moon keep shining above
Your smile and your love means so much to me.

The Princess and Jose clapped their hands and told Santiago he was so smart to remember this poem. The three friends talked about tomorrow. Princess Pumpkin spoke first. "We have to decide and plan a route. Maybe now that we are near the ocean, we might try to take a boat ride to a foreign port." "That should be exciting," said Santiago. Jose, who had spent most of his time on the golf course, loved the idea, as it certainly was a change.

"Tomorrow, we will ask around and look for a vessel to take us on an ocean ride." There we will be able to decide what course is best for us.

Suddenly, a voice was heard. "Six chickens, six chickens, six chickens." A beautiful bird appeared and repeated this over and over. The three friends looked amazed. There, sitting on the sand, on a beach ball, was the most beautiful parrot. The top of her head and her breast were a bright red. She had a white beak and her body was the most beautiful color green. She again repeated, "Six chickens, six chickens, six chickens."

Princess Pumpkin looked up at the parrot and greeted him. "Hello, Mr. Parrot. I am Princess Pumpkin and these are my friends, Santiago, and Jose. We are traveling together to find our future." The parrot looked up and spoke, "I flew away from home to find myself another family." "Why did you leave them?" asked Jose. "Well, Mama Rosa sent Ercole to shop for a chicken. There was a sale so he bought six chickens. Mama Rosa screamed at Ercole so many times that I had to leave."

Santiago spoke, "Would you care to come with us? We are searching for a large boat to take us out on the ocean to another land." The parrot was so excited to now have a new family. "Yes, yes, yes." Jose spoke, "Follow me. Your feathers are green and I wear a green golf cap. The bright color will keep us together so as not to lose each other. What is your name?" asked Jose. "Doo Da, is my name," said the parrot. He then perched himself on Jose's shoulder and said, "When you are ready, I am ready too." The sun was setting in the sky over the ocean waves and Santiago remembered another poem that he had read from his poem book back home.

THE SUN

The sun goes in
The sun comes out
Out from behind a big white cloud
It warms the earth
It brings bright light
The color yellow is the sun
Sometimes it turns to a red hot ball
Rises in the east and sets in the west
Warms the ocean and the waters blue
Makes you happy the whole year through
Melts the snow
And dries out the rain
Lives in the sky
A friend to all
Moves around the world and looks so small
Up in the heavens a beautiful ball.

The friends again clapped their hands and told Santiago they loved the poem. Jose, Doo Da and The Princess kissed Santiago and praised his poetry.

Morning was upon them. "It is time to continue on our way," said Santiago. "Let us search for a boat to take us to ride the waves of the ocean."

Walking along the beach, you could see boats of all sizes. Some were fishing boats. Some boats cruised the ocean. While on the watch for the right boat, a sign caught the attention of the group. It read, **COME ABOARD AND SAIL THE SEA. AN EXPERIENCE AWAITS YOU. FREE.**

A burly, rough looking man with a beard, and a red face stood on the boat. Santiago approached him. "Can you tell us about the trip you advertise? We do not have money but, we will all work for you." The man looked interested. "What can you do?" Santiago answered, "Well, I can scrub your deck." Princess Pumpkin then spoke, "I can cook your meals." Jose, the golfer, thought to himself, "What can I do?" "I can teach you all about the game of golf." Now, it was Doo Da's turn. "I can fly around and around and let you know all about the weather."

The burly man thought and finally realized that this was a comfortable solution for many of his problems. "I will have a maintenance man, a cook, a teacher, and a weatherman. This is better than money," and so he agreed to take them along with him. Captain Crook, thought to himself, this is surely a wacky group. He then spoke, "My name is Captain Crook, and I will give the orders. The name of my ship is the Neversink. Now, let us prepare for the trip."

Princess Pumpkin asked, "Where are we bound for?" Captain Crook replied, "We are on our way to Coober Pedy, the underground mining town in the outback of Australia. It has a zany charm, with caves and tunnels. Its' golf course has no trees, or greenery." Jose could not wait to see this.

This town has a great wall called the Dingo Fence. Everyone was so excited. "This trip sounds like fun and we will perhaps find our new future. It is time to start the voyage." Captain Crook instructed Doo Da to bring him a weather report as soon as possible.

Princess Pumpkin was taken down to the Galley to cook the meals for all. Captain Crook showed Santiago where all the equipment was stored to wash the deck and clean the ship.

Captain Crook steered the boat and planned the trip. He had crossed the ocean many times and was pleased with his good fortune of finding Santiago, Princess Pumpkin, Jose and Doo Da. As soon as his destination was completed and Doo Da would return with the weather report, the group would set sail for Coober Pedy in the outback of Australia.

Doo Da returned with the news that they might encounter some rough weather. A storm brought dark clouds and the ocean waves were rough. Only Captain Crook was familiar with the changes when out to sea.

The time was decided on when to leave and high noon was his decision. Santiago was scrubbing the deck. Princess Pumpkin's cooking created an aroma of home. Jose was drawing up a lesson plan for Captain Crook's golf time. Doo Da sat perched on Jose's shoulder. Captain Crook informed the wacky group that the ship was ready to start the journey.

One hour out, the waves were choppy and the winds were strong. Santiago was curious about the white caps on the waves. Jose asked Captain Crook if he could do some fishing at any time. "Then Princess Pumpkin could cook it for our dinner." Captain Crook laughed and explained to Jose, "the ship traveled too fast to stop and look for fish and we cannot fish in these deep waters for fear of sharks appearing. Sometimes we see dolphins at play jumping out of the water. They are friendly to people."

He also questioned Captain Crook about how much time it would take to reach Coober Pedy. The captain informed him that if the weather was calm, the trip would take at least one week at sea.

Princess Pumpkin wanted to know something about Coober Pedy. Captain Crook explained, "Coober Pedy – in Australia's outback, had lakes that were salty, and men with big arms and funny hats, cooked kangaroos and crocodiles. On my last trip to Coober Pedy I saw everyone in town carrying huge Mohawks. The men are ten feet tall covered with tattoos. The town has tunnels where reclusive residents live in caves. Coober Pedy's best feature is the field of hills housing some of the largest opal mines. That is what I search for and am returning to find; more opals. Some of the people live in underground caves. The 3500 residents that live in underground caves were former miners all searching for opals. Jose will be surprised to see a golf course without greenery, but instead enormous sand traps, which gives a whole new meaning to the game of golf. Signs are everywhere, **OPAL MINES, OPAL CAVES, OPAL FACTORIES AND THE OPAL CENTER.**" And now the rest remains to be seen. Captain Crook continued, "When we arrive at Coober Pedy you will see and meet many tourists searching for opals. Perhaps you too will want to search for opals."

Princess Pumpkin was so excited and so anxious to reach Coober Pedy. She looked up to the sky and down at the waves. She called out to Santiago, Jose, and Doo Da, "Come and see the sky. Hundreds of stars are shining tonight. Let us all wish upon a star and perhaps our dreams will come true." The friends stood together. The breezes were cool and the ocean was calm and the stars shone bright.

Each and everyone made their own wish. Captain Crook smiled, as he was happy to be with his new family.

It was the third day out to sea and all seemed to be perfect until Captain Crook saw another ship in the distance. They seemed to be coming in the direction of the Neversink. He watched carefully as the boat took on more speed. Pirates were known to be lurking on the high seas and perhaps in this vicinity. Captain Crook took out a huge shotgun. He was prepared to show his authority. He called upon Doo Da to fly as close to the other ship as possible and bring back some news. "Let me know if their cargo looks suspicious. We must be prepared for any problems that may arise." Captain Crook also alerted Santiago and Jose. We must hide Princess Pumpkin, as keeping a female on board should be kept a secret. Preparations were made to be friendly. We must protect ourselves from any unfriendly perpetrators.

Dark clouds were forming in the sky. Suddenly heavy rain started to fall. Captain Crook sent the crew below but he remained on deck waiting for the return of Doo Da. The winds become so fierce that the Neversink was covered with water as a result of the high waves. The ship tilted from side to side. Some lightening and thunder shook the ship. The sky lit up and Captain Crook had to steer and balance the vessel with the utmost of skill. Doo Da finally returned with the good news that the boat in the distance changed its' course away from the Neversink. A sigh of relief was shown by all. Princess Pumpkin came out of her hiding place. Santiago and Jose relaxed, and Captain Crook put away his rifle. The storm was subsiding and all those aboard were thinking of Coober Pedy once again.

Captain Crook had visited Coober Pedy several times. The Dingo Fence, as it was known, a 9,600 kilometer barrier, ran the length of the country from sea to sea. This sight would alert him when Coober Pedy was closer. Captain Crook called Coober Pedy a home under the range.

The fourth and fifth day on the sea, were calm and peaceful. The beautiful blue ocean with the white caps on the waves made the trip a ride of joy.

Captain Crook observed the Dingo Fence and knew that land was close by. He called to Santiago, Jose, Princess Pumpkin, Doo Da, and Duncan to be ready as they were nearing land. All were excited and impatient for the boat to dock on the shore of Coober Pedy. Captain Crook told the group that Cooper Pedy looked down in the dumps so as not to be too disappointed at first sight. Still, its' zany charm with the men with funny hats and big arms would be an interesting and different site for them to see. Captain Crook called the crew together. He made the announcement that Cooper Pedy was in sight and soon they would reach their destination. All were excited and looked forward to their new adventure.

Santiago stood on the helm of the ship. His heart pounded and his eyes filled with tears. He looked at the sea and saw the port of Cooper Pedy. Perhaps this experience would teach him how to live in a different place with new friends. He suddenly felt a hand on his shoulder. Jose was beside him and Princess Pumpkin took his hand in hers. Doo Da joined them and all watched as the ship entered the port of Cooper Pedy.

Captain Crook steered the ship and dropped his anchor into the water bringing the boat to a slow stop. A plank was extended onto the land and the crew stepped down. Just as Captain Crook said there were signs that read, **OPAL MINE, OPAL CAVE, BACKPACKS CAVE, OPAL FACTORY AND OPAL CENTER**.

Duncan wanted to know more about Coober Pedy. He asked Captain Crook if he knew the best mine to search in for the magical opal. Captain Crook knew all about the mines. He told Duncan, "the opal you speak of has a history of great magic. It has been said that it was found and is in the possession of the owner of the Red Sands Restaurant Night Club. Their men are ten feet tall, covered with tattoos and carry Mohawks of a huge size. They do not befriend strangers easily." Duncan felt frightened and hoped he could find the opal and its owner and perhaps could convince them to place the opal in Duncan's possession so he could return it to the Ohm.

There was the Red Sands Restaurant Night Club, a gas station, and a roadhouse Opal Shop. The roadhouse was underground; a sign read, THE GREAT WALL, THE DINGO FENCE, A 9,600 KILOMETER BARRIER RUNS THE LENGTH OF THE COUNTRY SEA TO SEA.

Captain Crook joined the group. "Well, you have three days to decide on your future. Meet me here at 1400 hours on the Neversink if you want to join me on the return trip. You are all on your own." He headed straight for the roadhouse and the warm beer. Santiago, Jose, and Princess Pumpkin decided to enter the caves and look for some opals. It is scenic until you remember you are standing on a gravel pit. After the three realized that digging for opals was not for them, they thought of another sight to see.

Jose was anxious to see the golf course with no trees or greenery to mark what is an enormous sand trap. Nine dreary holes were dug in dirt mounds of sand. The fairway was marked by a groove. Once inside players could tee off on a tiny piece of Astroturf they carry. Jose stared at this place and his first impression was disbelief. He then said, "This place gives a whole new meaning to golf."

The Opal Motel was not far away, so the team decided to rent a room and not go back to the Neversink until the designated time to leave. The following day brought information that the major finds are mainly in the museums. Many tourists come and go from all parts of the world to visit Cooper Pedy. Another attraction featured in all brochures is the Big Winch; Which turns out to be just that, a Big Winch.

When on land Duncan boarded his trusty bicycle and was ready to drive to through the city and find the Red Sands Restaurant, and perhaps the owner of the magical opal. "Where are you all going when you get to town?" asked Duncan. Princess Pumpkin, Santiago and Jose, all said they would go to the mines and search for opals.

Duncan separated from the crew and decided to search on his own. The bicycle would speed his search. He decided to visit the Red Sands Restaurant and Night Club as his first stop. He said goodbye to all and started his journey in this weird town. Roaming around the town he saw the Night Club. He dismounted his bicycle and chained it to a pole. He entered a dark, noisy and scary looking area. Suddenly, two ten feet tall men approached Duncan, one on either side of him. They were residents of Coober Pedy who were covered in tattoos. Finally one spoke, "Who are you and what are you looking for?" said one man to Duncan. " I must speak to the main man," said Duncan. "We are all main men. What is this about?" "I am Duncan from Talkatoo Cavern where animals and birds of all kinds live together peacefully and have voices to speak to each other. I have been sent on a mission by our Ohm who is the elder, to search for a magical opal and return it to Talkatoo Cavern. This opal can determine the future of Talkatoo Cavern. My mission here is peaceful and I hope to be successful." The two huge men held tightly on to Duncan. At a large round table sat men drinking warm beer. Loud music played as the giants were deciding what to do with Duncan. Luck, good and bad was what brought people to Coober Pedy. Duncan hoped his luck was good. Finally one of the men spoke. "We must take you to an underground 17 room cave where the main man lives and has more opals than anyone else. Perhaps he owns the opal you are searching for." Duncan then spoke, "My bicycle is outside and it can ride us to the destination you have mentioned." The two men agreed.

Duncan's bike had two extension seats and enough room for the two men. They all boarded the bicycle and gave directions to the underground mansion. They sped away through the streets and tunnels of Coober Pedy. Soon arriving at a huge cave, Duncan's eyes lit up. He had never seen anything this size.

As they entered bugles could be heard. There, sitting on a thrown like chair was the tallest man Duncan had ever seen. Tattoos covered his entire body. He had a tomahawk and wore a wide brimmed hat. He stared at Duncan. "What brings you to Coober Pedy?" he asked. "My name is Duncan and I am on a mission to retrieve the magical opal for my friends at Talkatoo Cavern. I have been informed of your great collection of opals and am hoping you possess the magical opal. I do not have money to buy the opal but if you can present this opal to me our Ohm will grant you long life and good luck for all at Coober Pedy."

The Main Man stood erect from his chair and walked to a wall full of boxes. He bowed before the wall and pushed it open. Beyond this wall was a huge door. There the Main Man opened the door and a burst of light blinded Duncan. It was the magical Opal mounted on a steal frame. The beauty of the opal was astonishing. "Because you wish to use the opal to preserve Talkatoo Cavern, which creates good deeds, I am happy to grant you your wish, on one condition." Duncan asked, "What is it?" "Never let this out of your sight. The Ohm must protect this gift with all his power and remember the magical value of this stone. It can bring life. It can bring death." The Main Man lifted the jewel and placed it in a box. Smoke surrounded the opal protecting it from harm. "Now go and bring this gift to The Ohm and use this gift wisely."

Duncan thanked the Main Man and left hurriedly. He placed the box on his bicycle and sped back to Captain Crook's ship.

This trip was not what the Amigos had expected. What were they thinking, a new future? The Amigos decided to visit an opal mine. Perhaps they could be lucky. A tall dark man in charge, volunteered to give them supplies to dig and find some opals. A sharp instrument similar to a knife, a hammer like iron, and a small shovel were the tools of the trade. There were many people also in the area digging for opals. Santiago chose an area and Princess Pumpkin bent on her knees waiting to start the dig. The sharp tool was placed inside the earth and all started to hammer and dig as hard as they could. The first hole did not show any promise of opals, so Jose decided to move down on a slanted hill and try his efforts again. This was not an easy task. After some time passed, the group who was working as hard as they could, decided to leave without finding any opals. "Let us visit the other sites of Coober Pedy," said Santiago. "The museum might be an interesting place to visit." They caroused around until they found the museum. The inside was interesting and strange looking. Objects of art were not familiar to them. They decided to leave and head back to the boat.

Santiago thought of his nice warm and cozy house. Princess Pumpkin was starting to miss the farm. Jose wanted some green grass to lose his ball. Doo Da was tired of flying around and checking out the weather.

Santiago spoke, "Maybe, we ought to hurry back to Captain Crook's ship to make sure we return to our homes." Princess Pumpkin and Jose and Doo Da nodded their heads as if to agree. Roaming the world was not what they were really searching for but they had met and made new friends and this made this experience a treasure to remember.

Meanwhile Princess Pumpkin, Santiago and Jose were also boarding the ship returning from their search. Duncan asked, "did you find some opals?" "Oh yes," they chimed in, "and we are very happy." Just then Captain Crook appeared. It is time to set sail. Captain Crook was content with the time he spent at Coober Pedy. He bought supplies and food for the trip and drank his warm beer. He renewed his old friendship and made new ones.

Princess Pumpkin, Santiago and Jose now owned some opals and had such an exciting vacation. Duncan had completed his mission once again and now would return to Talkatoo Cavern to deliver the Magical Opal to The Ohm.

~

Damanhur and Duncan's Search For The Temple of Humankind

Duncan's amazing bicycle had bright lights and wheels of steel. The handlebars were made from tree trunks. The motor which attached to the engine, made it fly the fastest speed imaginable.

When Duncan returned from Talkatoo Cavern a message awaited him, from The Ohm. He had delivered the magical opal to The Ohm. The Ohm contacted Duncan with another request for a new journey. It was a trip to Damanhur in Italy, the community practicing spirituality and the future of humankind. The Ohm had requested for Duncan to search for the future of peace, The Book of Rules that held the laws to The Temple of Humankind. The Blue Temple is the oldest and used for meditation. The Book, held by The Baron, reveals all and must be returned to Talkatoo Cavern.

The Ohm had instructed Duncan to search Damanhur for The Baron. The Baron was a person of great wisdom and culture who originated the Blue Temple. Duncan had in his possession the Wikipedia, and turned to it for information. There he found his answers about how to reach Damanhur. High speed straight ahead.

Duncan boarded his bicycle, snapped his helmet to his head, and quickly pressed the button that read, flying machine. This elevated his bicycle into the air. Flying through space thrilled Duncan. He spoke into the Escape

Button requesting directions to the Temple of Humankind. A voice replied, "Italy is our destination. It is shaped like a boot, and at the sole deep in the boot, in a valley lays the Temple of Humankind." Duncan's excitement at hearing the voice behind the Escape Button forced him to shift his gears and increase his speed. His heart raced and his breath quickened with anticipation. Soon he would be on a new journey and search for The Baron.

Duncan's bike sped ahead. He sometimes felt a hand on his shoulder protecting him from harm. He looked up to the sky and asked for strength and a safe arrival to find The Baron. The wind against Duncan's face told him that he was protected and he would soon arrive at his destination. The clouds he passed in the sky seemed to be friendly and talk to him and say this journey would soon be completed.

Below, Duncan saw mountains and valleys. His bike was headed for the ground. High cathedral buildings were beneath him. Duncan was sure this was the land where the Blue Temple of Humankind would be and he could search for The Baron. In a short time Duncan landed. A group of people approached him. "Who are you and what are you doing here." "I am Duncan from Talkatoo Cavern," he replied. "I am looking for the Blue Temple of Humankind. I want to speak with The Baron. Am I in Damanhur?" asked Duncan. "Yes, and we are the welcoming committee. Some people come here to meditate and others to visit. After visiting, many of the people remain and live here. We are a unique and happy community. There is much to see. We have beautiful temples with historic artwork. We also have lectures about our historical tunnels and museums. We have The Hall of Water, the Hall of Earth, and the Hall of Metals."

Duncan was interested in the story of Damanhur. He could return to Talkatoo Cavern with new ideas and information that might improve the growth and lifestyle of Talkatoo Cavern. "I would like to know all about Damanhur before my search for The Baron," said Duncan. "We have businesses here at Damanhur; bakeries, a cheese dairy, and a laboratory for food and agriculture for tourism."

"The Baron requests that all who visit Damanhur learn about our culture and customs so when they return to their own country they will spread the word of humankind. We have artists and craftsman and woman of Dh-crea who integrate tei with full respect."

"Valchieseella is the origin of the Temple of Humankind. The center promotes sound trade from food and herbal preparation. We have given you the short story of Damanhur. Perhaps in the future you will return with your friends and enjoy our land."

Duncan explained to the committee, "I was sent by the senior elder, The Ohm, from Talkatoo Cavern, as our scrolls have instructed us to learn of your culture and wisdom. Now I must try to meet with The Baron," said Duncan. "Can you direct me to him?" A committee member stepped forward and volunteered to take Duncan to The Baron. "You must come with me in my Damanhur machine as no foreign objects can pass through the gates to The Baron. Duncan agreed to accompany the committee member. He asked, "What is your name?" "My name is Rocco. I am a trusted friend of The Baron."

The weather was warm and sunny and Duncan was excited and tried to learn as much as he could. He looked around at all the houses and buildings. Rocco started up his machine and Duncan held on tightly as they started the ride The streets were cobblestone, causing bumps in the road The ride was short. They stopped at a stone house with gates of steel. The guards that stood at the gate knew Rocco and waved him on into the compound.

As Duncan was ushered into a room, there were steps leading down into a tunnel. Suddenly, Duncan found himself blindfolded. When his blindfold was lifted there before him sat a man wrapped in a large cape. Duncan immediately asked, "Is this The Baron? Sir, I am Duncan from Talkatoo Cavern. I represent our senior elder, The Ohm who has an mportant request. Talkatoo houses animals and creatures of ıll kinds all possessing a talking voice. Our life style is similar to yours here at The Temple in Damanhur. The Ohm s aware that you possess the book of rules and regulations or humankind. He is in need of the book to continue the elationship of all the animals at Talkatoo Cavern."

"I am The Baron, and I have in my possession The Book hat you request. It has been in the possession of The Temple or many years and has been helpful in keeping order here at The Temple. If I can be of service to The Ohm and help spread the joy of Humankind I am at The Ohm's service."

The Baron hidden under his cape did not divulge the nagic of his cape. "Come Duncan, come fly with me to the unnel that holds The Book and many other important issues." Duncan stepped under The Baron's cape. The Baron wrapped Duncan and himself securely inside the cape. Before Duncan could take another breath, his feet were off the ground and The Baron held him tightly. They soared into the air like a speed of light and disappeared up to a mountaintop. "Where ıre we?" asked Duncan. "This is the Mountain of Hope," eplied The Baron. "Here we hold treasures worth more than gold. Scriptures and scrolls written by our ancestors and essons of hope and love are in the Mountain. Precious words of wondrous and happy thoughts are our future for the Temple of Humankind." At the top of the mountain an arrow appeared in the sand. "Follow the arrow and you will discover, The Book." Duncan followed the arrows. A burning bush of red leaves appeared. "Search the bush," said The Baron, "and you will find The Book." Duncan pulled the branches apart and found The Book hidden amongst the leaves. "Sir Baron, I have found it. I have found it!" shouted Duncan and held it close to his body. Duncan looked around for The Baron, but he was nowhere to be seen. "How will I return to Talkatoo?" shouted Duncan. Duncan was frightened and wished for his trusty bicycle. Once again he felt the hand on his shoulder. There before him was his bicycle. He placed The Book inside his Duffel Bag. Duncan boarded his bike. He thought of the Blue Temple and Damanhur and he then knew the meaning and power of Humankind, and this inspired him for his trip back to Talkatoo Cavern.

FREEBIRD

~

A DISCOVERY OF THE PLANET OF AIR AND LIGHT

Duncan awoke to feel a tapping on his shoulder. During all of his trips he felt that a warm comforting feeling held him and protected him. Suddenly, his feeling came to life. A voice spoke to him. "I am your invisible friend. I am a Freebird and I am here to protect you. You are destined to fly with me to the Planet of Light, the Circle of Air, and the Bubble of Sound. These trips will educate and strengthen your mind and body so that you can return with knowledge to share with all.

"Your trusty wheel mobile will lift you to the highest space in the sky. Let us not wait any longer. The winds are strong which helps us ascend more easily." Duncan was always ready for any new adventure. He thought to himself, this trip may help me bring the gift of knowledge to my friends at Talkatoo Cavern.

Duncan pressed the button ascend on his trusty wheel mobile bicycle. With the help of the strong gust of wind, Duncan was once again flying in space.

Freebird, although invisible, could be felt by Duncan. His presence was always with him. Bursts of light beyond the clouds excited Duncan. "Perhaps we are nearing the Planet of Light," he said. Streaks of colors lit up the sky. Duncan was anxious to enter the planet and discover its secrets of light. Perhaps here he could find the true wonders of the planet. Flying high, Duncan felt free as a bird. He noticed a sparkle of light coming closer to him. "I wonder if this is the Planet of Light." As he flew higher he felt surrounded. There on either side of him were star shaped lights. Duncan knew he had entered the Planet of Light.

Duncan called upon Freebird. "Are we here yet?" asked Duncan. "We are entering the planet," replied Freebird. "Are you familiar with these twinkling stars?" asked Duncan. "Yes," said Freebird. "They are the lights you see in the sky when the sun goes down and the day turns into night. The large cluster of stars is called the Big Dipper." Duncan was intent on remembering important facts to bring back to Talkatoo Cavern. "What else can you tell me about this planet?" asked Duncan. "Well, dancing with the stars is an important event," said Freebird. "Turning the lights in the stars off and on is also important, and if the lights remain off, the darkness remains below." Duncan was impressed but was ready to leave this planet and search for the Circle of Air.

Leaving the Planet of Light, when flying through space, a circular look-alike body approached Duncan. It enveloped Duncan and his wheel mobile. This round Circle of Air turned Duncan around and around, upside down, swaying from one side to the other.

Duncan held on tightly to his bicycle. The turning and twisting made Duncan dizzy. He reached out to feel for Freebird and hoped he was there to protect him. Soon the motion lessened and Duncan was in the center of the Circle of Air. "What happened?" asked Duncan to Freebird. "You have entered the Circle of Air, and now know what it is. Fog and wind, cold and salty air made it difficult for nature and planted trees to survive here. It constitutes an atmosphere condition. You cannot see it, you cannot feel it but you cannot hold it. Let us leave and locate the Bubble of Sound."

Traveling ahead, small shaped circles of all sizes appeared. Offsprings of Bubbles from larger Bubbles were detaching themselves and swirling around. Duncan asked, "What made the small Bubbles detach from the parent Bubble?" "The offspring had to be ready to leave their parents Bubble and spread out on their own." Small Bubbles had rainbows in the center of each one. The look of a Bubble was fragile. Suddenly, a huge parent Bubble appeared perhaps searching for her child-like baby Bubble.

Duncan was enthralled with the sight he saw. He forgot to steer his mobile and suddenly started to descend toward the ground. He really wanted to stay in that area where all the Bubbles seemed to accumulate. A parent Bubble seemed to be following Duncan. He came so close to Duncan that he almost burst and disappeared. Duncan made sure he did not hit into the parent Bubble. At close range to the large Bubble, Duncan could see small tears run down the face of the Bubble. The sadness of losing its baby Bubbles caused the parent Bubble to shed some tears.

Air is mainly composed of nitrogen, oxygen, and argon, which together constitutes the major gases of the atmosphere. The time spent in the atmosphere and looking around at the sky and the stars and the Bubbles caused Duncan to realize the importance of family. "I can bring all of these wonders to my friends in Talkatoo Cavern."

The clouds were darkening and Duncan could see a storm brewing up ahead. He called and motioned to Freebird, "Do you think it is time to return to our own planet?" Freebird informed Duncan, the sound he now heard were planet sounds. The action from detaching Bubbles caused some noises. He also told Duncan that the hills on the mountain and rivers below were not just to be taken as scenery. The mountains and rivers had a job to do. The greenery around the mountain, such as trees and bushes were a haven for animals. Birds made nests called homes and the waters in lakes housed the fish. "I have some friends that live down in the mountain," said Freebird. "If you look closely as we descend, you will see the interaction of all the animals and birds. Many depend on each other for food and safety."

Duncan listened carefully to Freebird. His friend forever was attached to his shoulder. Duncan once more thought of all the places he had been, all the people he had met, and the fun and happiness he felt. He never wanted to stop exploring the world. He would search the world for interesting people and different cultures. "This is my future," said Duncan. He turned to look for Freebird, but he was nowhere to be seen. Duncan knew he was not alone. Freebird would always be with him. Duncan said aloud, "I can't see you Freebird, but I know you are always with me. I am never alone."

THE MAGICAL WORLD THROUGH DUNCAN'S EYES

Duncan was startled from a deep sleep. A tap on his shoulder was from his invisible companion Freebird. When he spoke to Duncan and said, "Duncan do you believe in magic?" Duncan rubbed his eyes, scratched his head and thought for a moment, "I'm not sure. Do you mean real magic?" Freebird knew Duncan was different and special when he asked him this question. "I mean real magic with real live visible subjects. You see I know all about imagination. Since I fly all around and all over the world and am a descendent of the bird family I can take you on a magical trip only where birds fly."

Duncan always saw the world through magic. He wanted to see and learn magic. With his Duffel Bag attached to his body and his magic wheel mobile bicycle, his invisible friend Freebird on his shoulder, Duncan felt he could explore the world.

Freebird told Duncan to close his eyes, dream of magical thoughts and upon opening his eyes a vision would appear. Suddenly floating high in the sky was a hot air balloon that kept coming closer and closer to Duncan. As soon as it reached Duncan, Freebird appeared and told Duncan to place his magical wheel mobile on the air balloon and he would now experience the ride of his life.

Duncan raised his arms above his head as if to balance

himself. He boarded the hot air balloon, and as the balloon soared high above the clouds he felt free and weightless. He knew the feeling now of total freedom. At that moment he realized that riding on the balloon was like floating on air. Duncan wondered what surprises were in his future and what he would see; Perhaps a new land. Duncan felt the magic that Freebird had promised him and was ready for his exciting, heavenly, peaceful, serene and amazing new adventure.

Little did Duncan realize that this new experience would be so exciting. Up in the air balloon, a cluster of stars known as galaxies were visible. "Do you know anything about stargazing?" asked Freebird. All the stars in the heavens are clustered together. Just as all people are clustered together in the world. A typical galaxy contains billions of individual stars.

Our sun belongs to a cluster of two hundred billion stars called the Milky Way, which has the shape of a giant spiral. All the galaxies are moving away from earth at a high speed.

As the balloon ascended, the daytime was changing to dusk and this was the best time to observe all the wonders in the sky. "You know," said Duncan, "it is best to observe the sky in the darkness. The most interesting part of the sky is the southern section because it changes most when the sky turns overhead."

Freebird was such a good listener. Although he was an invisible friend to Duncan, he enjoyed Duncan's enthusiasm. "You see," said Duncan, "I visited the Planetarium with my dad. There you see the sky and its' family."

The balloon floated high in the sky. Duncan was able to see the world below him, houses and lakes, rivers and streams. "Perhaps we could live here in the sky forever," said Duncan.

As the night turned into day, the sun came out from behind a cloud and warmed the air.

After some time it seemed to Duncan that the balloon was descending toward land. Duncan spoke to Freebird, "I wonder where we are." We have traveled so many miles. Now the balloon was touching the ground. Duncan heard unfamiliar sounds. Then he saw kangaroos, elephants, animals of many kinds and wild looking species. The area looked like a habitat for animals. They scurried about at the sight of the balloon. Freebird knew all about these animals. This area is a home for old animals such as elephants, tigers, lions and kangaroos. Duncan was amazed at what he saw. The story is said that these are old animals that cannot take care of themselves anymore in the wild forest and have several people who watch over them. They feed them and love them.

Now it is time to ascend our balloon again. We have much to see. Climbing high in the sky the puffy clouds resembling cotton balls felt like old friends protecting the balloon.

Duncan looked down and on the peak of a huge mountain stood what looked like a castle. He turned to Freebird to ask what was below on that mountain but before he knew it the balloon was descending. Upon landing Duncan looked around but there were no people to be seen. He decided to step off the balloon and enter the castle. He searched around and discovered that this castle was made of glass. Perhaps a king, queen, or princess lives here. As he looked for an entrance into the castle, a creature resembling a horse appeared. A horse with large wings and a beautiful body approached Duncan. It was a flying horse. Duncan stood amazed at this site and spoke. "Who are you? Do you live here at the castle and do you have a name?" The horse shook his head from side to side, spread his wings and sped away causing the glass castle to shake. It saddened him to see the horse disappear.

Duncan realized he must return to the balloon and seriously think all about his friends, his experiences, and the places he had been. He boarded the balloon hoping Freebird would appear. Duncan sometimes felt lonely and wanted to talk about his new experiences, and although Freebird was available he needed real live friends. Perhaps in the near future he would meet someone.

As the balloon floated high in the sky, the clouds were close to Duncan and he reached out to touch one. He then took out a large piece of colored paper from his Duffel Bag and folded it many times until it took the shape of a kite. He attached a string to the kite that he found in his bag and gradually extended it up into the sky. It flew up higher than the balloon and Duncan watched as it disappeared.

There was much to watch and do while in the balloon. Suddenly, a strong wind caused the balloon to sway and shake. A huge plane was nearby and Duncan waved as it passed him. I want to pilot a plane someday Duncan thought to himself.

The most beautiful sight Duncan experienced while on his trip home was a rainbow covering half the sky. The blue and gold colors on the rainbow seemed like a mysterious miracle.

Duncan felt so fortunate to be close to a different world. The galaxies, the moon, the sun, and the clouds, they all have a reason and a purpose to live in the sky, but now it was time to return to earth. Before he did, Duncan wanted to do something more exciting. Perhaps he could walk on the moon. He would walk in space and leave a note with his name to be the first young boy to walk on the moon. Duncan wished Freebird would appear so he could tell him of his dream. He closed his eyes and concentrated on seeing Freebird. Suddenly, Freebird appeared. "Are you looking for me?" Freebird's voice made Duncan happy. "I have a dream to walk on the moon. Can you help me my friend?" There was no answer. This was a difficult task. Freebird thought, "how could I disappoint Duncan? Well Duncan, your wish is my command. Soon the moon will eclipse and that will give you the opportunity to jump onto the moon. I must stay here with the balloon so it does not leave without you. Let us watch carefully and fly as high as we can and closer to the moon." Duncan was ready. He watched and waited till the balloon climbed higher and higher. The air was clear, the sun was bright, and in the distance another plane could be seen. "Duncan, Duncan," called Freebird, "The time is now. You must leave your mobile with me as your walk on the moon can only be step by step with the weightlessness of your feet to guide you on your walk." Duncan concentrated on all instructions that Freebird directed him to follow. The moon was in front of the air balloon. Duncan was excited and thrilled as he stepped onto the moon. His body was light and he walked slowly. There he saw an object of interest. A flag was blowing in the breeze. Duncan approached and tied his flag with a note attached to the existing flag. He turned and walked around sort of floating on air. He looked down at the floor of the moon and saw a stone and decided to bring this back to Talkatoo Cavern. Duncan heard Freebird call. "We must go now as our balloon is ready to descend." Duncan looked around and waved goodbye, boarded the balloon and started his trip back home. "This had been the thrill of a lifetime and so educational," said Duncan. He turned to talk to Freebird, but Freebird was nowhere in sight. His invisible friend would surely return someday.

DUNCAN AND HIS DUFFEL BAG IN THE PETRIFIED FOREST

A new journey was to begin for Duncan. When reading the Book of Good Deeds, Duncan found a letter hidden between the pages addressed to him giving him instructions for a new adventure.

The Forbidden Forest, the oldest forest housing petrified trees from years gone by was his new mission. A message from "The Ohm" of Talkatoo Cavern had reached him. Talkatoo Cavern, the haven for animals and birds of all kinds; the home of Wally-the-Walligator, Blue Footed Boobie, and Angora the cat, were all Duncan's best and devoted friends and once again in need of his help.

A swarm of bees were overtaking all of Talkatoo Cavern, spreading disease in our beloved Talkatoo. All the inhabitants are sick and in need of help. The secrets of directing the bees back to their hives lies in the forest of old and petrified trees.

Each tree possesses a secret answer and a search must begin immediately to reach the forest and save Talkatoo Cavern. Duncan once again was chosen for his past success in solving the problems of Talkatoo Cavern.

Duncan did not sleep that night as he was planning a way for the bees in Talkatoo Cavern to become friendly and perhaps return for pollination. He knew he could not attempt a trip on his bicycle or his hot air balloon. He must arrive at the forest in an enclosed ship so as when returning to Talkatoo he would be protected from an attack of the bees.

Duncan once again called upon his trusty friend Freebird. Freebird was his invisible companion. He was smart and reliable. Duncan turned his head to the right, rubbed his shoulder, and wished for Freebird to appear. Little did Duncan know that Freebird was on a mission far across the ocean. Duncan's vibes sent out to Freebird were strong and magical. A connection from his thoughts, a mysterious attachment to Freebird from Duncan could not be explained to any one individual. Their friendship was intangible and wishing always made it so.

Before daybreak, Duncan felt Freebird on his shoulder. Duncan spoke, "I must find the Petrified Forest and find the Tree of Knowledge. There in this tree, we will find our answer to save Talkatoo Cavern, its environment, and preserve our beautiful Talkatoo for all the talking animals that have a home." Freebird spoke, "Let us contact our friend the Bubble."

The spaceship that the Bubble had once appeared in when Duncan was on another trip was now what Duncan and Freebird were in need of. Freebird put on his magical hat with its mystical powers and started to contact the Bubble.

The windmill on his hat started to spin around.

Freebird shouted, "Come in friend." Freebird repeated, "It is Freebird here over and out." The Bubble with its huge round bulging eyes and antennas on the top of its head, a round circular body, started to tingle with joy when his longtime friend Freebird was blogging him. "Connecting! Connecting!" A sharp bright light, an electric shock, passed through the Bubble. His antennas were alive. Freebird spoke, "We must use your spaceship to travel to the Petrified Forest. Our mission is imperative. Duncan has been called upon once again to save Talkatoo Cavern. The Cavern is under attack by a band of bees. They are attacking and stinging all the animals. Without hesitation the Bubble replied, "I am on my way. My Geiger counter will find you wherever you are." Like a shot of electricity, the Bubble took off.

East or West, North or South, the Bubble was so amazing. He could locate a destination immediately. His take off filled the air with streams of smoke. Sitting on top of a mountain, Duncan waited with Freebird. He tried to signal the Bubble. The Bubble circled the mountain, saw Duncan, and while the friends waited patiently, the Bubble soon landed safely. He greeted Duncan and Freebird.

They soon boarded the spaceship and the friends would now search for the forest of petrified trees.

From high in the sky, visibility was clear and after

several miles of traveling, some trees could be distinguishable. Duncan called out, "I see a clump of trees without green leaves. This must be the Petrified Forest. Let us now descend."

The Bubble swerved the space ship, flew up and down, surveying the land below. Many trees were visible and different looking, old, and showing bare branches. Deep in the forest was a space and empty section of land suitable for the Bubble to park. The Bubble set his sight and soon the space ship was on the ground. The three friends were excited and eager to start on their journey.

A bumpy landing was endured but finally the Bubble came to a halt. The three friends stepped down and looked around at an amazing site of dried and huge trees, which surrounded them. The trees in the forest were old. Each tree was different. Duncan was informed when he read the message in the Book of Good Deeds that behind each tree lies a message. A message of hope for the saving of Talkatoo Cavern. Some of the trees had windows that opened and closed when magic words were spoken. At night the swaying of the branches created a whistle that could be heard, sometimes frightening Duncan, Freebird, and the Bubble. Freebird spoke, "Come let us tour the land and search the trees. Time is of the essence." The trees were scattered in different sections. Duncan approached a tree with a see-through window. He peered into the window and suddenly a flash of light blinding Duncan for the moment, caused him to lose his balance and fall backwards. Duncan was astonished and decided to be more careful in the future. Suddenly, a voice could be heard resonating from the tree. "Who are you and why are you here?" Duncan who had previously experienced talking animals, now experienced a talking tree. "I come as a friend in search of an answer for a good deed for all my friends in Talkatoo Cavern, where talking animals live. A swarm of bees have invaded Talkatoo and threaten their existence. We must settle in a peaceful and friendly manner. Perhaps you can help me find the Tree of Knowledge and Wisdom." Suddenly, the door on the face of the tree opened and a yellow, wrinkled and creased paper map was handed to Duncan. The tree talked, "Follow the road reading courage and friendship. There stands an old Sequoia Tree. Now you must solve the mysteries on the map." The door slammed shut and Duncan was bewildered. Freebird, Duncan and the Bubble stared at the map. The instructions were confusing but they decided to concentrate and figure out their destination. A dark line pointed to a triangle on the map. Duncan opened his Duffel Bag. Perhaps an idea may sprout while rumbling through his belongings. His trusty flashlight lit up his Duffel Bag. Suddenly, that beam of light purple in color pointed to an arrow on the map. A signal of hope appeared. There at the far end of the map was a clue. Three dots pointed to a line, which resembled a fork in the road. Duncan was excited. This had to point to the old Sequoia Tree. Searching the map for more clues, an odd shaped rock appeared which took them closer and closer to their destination. There at the bottom of the map was a lake with a waterfall. We now have enough information to start our search for the Sequoia tree. Duncan was the first in line as the Bubble and Freebird followed. The road twisted and turned, broken bushes and branches made it difficult for walking. Freebird called out to Duncan, "I see a huge odd shaped rock ahead. Be careful not to make any noise as there might be a foreign object ahead hiding behind the rock." Slowly and carefully they approached the rock but all was still. Duncan looked at the map once again. From this point we must search behind the waterfall. The three dots will form the triangle and the old Sequoia tree should come into sight. Duncan's feet were suddenly immersed in water. Water seemed to be all around Duncan and the Bubble. Freebird flew onto Duncan's shoulder. The waterfall created a rush of water and threw them off balance. Groping and holding on to each other, Duncan held the Bubble and slowly the water started to recede in front of them, and there a view of the largest Sequoia tree imaginable came into sight. A rumbling of the earth beneath their feet frightened Duncan. Through a crack in the tree, fireballs bolted into the air. A voice could be heard, "Do not come any closer. This is sacred ground." Duncan's knees were shaking. Words could not come out of his mouth. His body was frozen. Fear had overtaken his mind. He thought "What can I do?" Suddenly, Freebird flew around the tree circling it and started to sing. He was trying to charm the tree, and after a few minutes the voice in the tree could be heard again. "Why are you here?" Duncan although trembling, explained their mission. "Our friends at Talkatoo Cavern have been invaded by a swarm of bees, and The Ohm of Talkatoo has sent us to you. The Book of Good Deeds says that you have the magic power and the knowledge to save Talkatoo Cavern." The tree spoke, "You are good friends and shall be rewarded. There is a flower called Flora Dora hidden in one of my tallest branches. Break off the tallest branch and at the highest point of the tree you will find Flora Dora. Return this flower back to Talkatoo and the bees will follow you and pollinate.

Freebird was excited. He could fly as high as a kite and find the branch. They all thanked Mr. Sequoia tree as Freebird would now fly above the ground and find the branch with the flower called Flora Dora. In seconds, Freebird was out of site. Duncan and the Bubble waited and hoped for Freebird to succeed. Not moments later, Freebird appeared with the branch and the flower. It was time to start their journey back to the space ship. "Our good deed will be recorded, and when we return with the flower, happiness and peace will reign once again at Talkatoo Cavern.

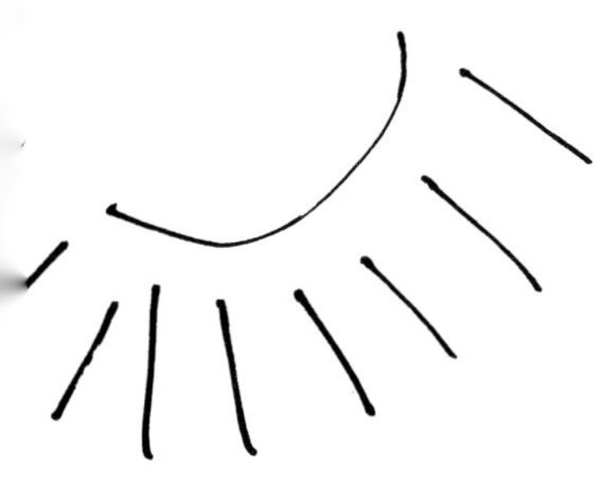

About The Author

Trude Brooks, aka Fannie's Girl, is a senior presently living in Florida. The author was born and raised in Brooklyn, New York. Her mother emigrated from Russia, her father was born in the United States. The experience of family life created stories of love, happy times and family relationships.

Her book "**Outside My Window**" is a result of years of admiring the outside activity of children, the beauty of nature and the seasons changes in the weather and the atmosphere.

The author's newest adventure stories for children "**Duncan and His Duffel Bag, A Collection of Seven Short Stories**", portrays her love of adventure, discovery of new places, and teaching children through a story.

"Such authors as Robert Louis Stevenson, Emily Dickinson and Louisa May Alcott have inspired me. It is my belief that children's literature is the key to education. My first serious introduction to poetry was a book of poems given to me, as a gift, by my first grade teacher, thus inspiring me to write."

About The Artist

The Little Artist in the Big Apple Born and raised in New York, the Artist earned a master of Arts Degree in Therapeutic Techniques and Education, cum laude, from the college of New Rochelle, and a Master of Fine Arts Degree, summa cum laude from C.W. Post College, Long Island University. Her works have been exhibited both in the United States and internationally. She has taught art to children of all ages. She illustrated **"Outside My Window"**, and **"The Adventure of Duncan and His Duffel Bag in Talkatoo Cavern"**, each a collaborative piece created with her mother. In addition to being an artist she is a well known specialist in Human Resources and a Vice President and Director of Human Resources for a major corporation.

QUESTIONS AND ANSWERS

1. WHAT STARTED YOU WRITING FOR CHILDREN?

Writing is a personal way of expressing my interpretations of all, and everything connected to the development of children.

2. WHAT IS THE EASIEST PART AND WHAT IS THE MOST DIFFICULT PART OF WRITING?

The easiest part of writing is that I find it to be a very pleasant experience. I find myself smiling at times when I write because of feeling so good about Mother Nature or situations that remain with me always. I never find writing difficult as I enjoy these moments alone with my stories and the characters I invent.

3. WHAT IS THE PRIMARY MOTIVATION FOR BECOMING A WRITER?

My primary reason for writing is the experiences it brings into my life. My imagination takes me to places where beautiful things brighten my time of day and this belongs solely to me. I do not have to share these moments.

4. PLEASE TELL US ABOUT YOUR BOOKS.

"Outside My Window" is a collection of 28 descriptive poems about pets, friendships and relationships illustrated. My poetry educates, sensitizes, and delights a young mind. From this poetry book three characters were created; Wally-the-Walligator, Blue Footed Boobie, and Angora, The Angry Cat. In "The Adventures of Duncan and His Duffel Bag in Talkatoo Cavern" they are Duncan's friends and this is where he develops relationships with animals who talk, learn about how to work through new and challenging situations, and begin his exciting adventures into new places. Duncan becomes lost in their home of Talkatoo Cavern. My most recent book, "The Adventures of Duncan and His Duffel Bag, A Collection of Seven Short Stories, takes Duncan's adventures to new and exciting places around the globe.

5. HOW MUCH TIME DO YOU SAY YOU SPEND WRITING YOUR BOOKS?

To complete my thoughts and put it into writing and develop the different chapters takes several years, or maybe it is a lifetime of living, images, and envisioning a variety of elements. "Outside My Window" is an observation of experiencing some personal moments and some that are created.

6. WHAT PROMPTED YOU TO WRITE FOR CHILDREN?

My thoughts are that every new generation of children offers our society the opportunity of forging ahead. For the success of our future, our children are our most important assets.

7. WHAT HAVE BEEN THE REACTIONS OF PARENTS AND TEACHERS AFTER READING YOUR BOOKS?

The reactions and sales of the book have been overwhelmingly positive. Teachers are delighted and I quote, "I will love reading these to my class". Parents declare their pleasure in reading these short stories to their children. The short stories are very popular and offer a novel approach to shared reading activities between parents and children in our fast paced society with little extra time.

8. DO YOU THINK THAT BOOKS COULD MAKE A DIFFERENCE OR CHANGE THE WAY A CHILD MIGHT THINK AFTER ABSORBING THE SUBJECT MATTER?

Yes, within each story there are many messages to teach children about friendships, evaluating and working through different challenging situations, and learning how to "figure out" the best way to positively handle things, negotiate, and "get along" with others.

9. DO YOU HAVE A FAVORITE STORY IN YOUR COLLECTION OF WORKS?

Each poem or story has a different meaning or message which is important. As a mother with children, each one is loved the same, but each one stands out in a different way.

10. DO YOU RESEARCH THE TOPICS FOR YOUR BOOKS?

Yes, I research places that Duncan travels to on the Internet and I, like Duncan, are particularly fond of the Wikipedia.

11. DOES WRITING PRESENT YOU WITH CHALLENGES?

Any writing presents a challenge. You have to think about what you want to say and where you want to place the characters